Anthony Gilbert and The Murder Room

>>> This title is part of The Murder Room, our series dedicated to making available out-of-print or hard-to-find titles by classic crime writers.

Crime fiction has always held up a mirror to society. The Victorians were fascinated by sensational murder and the emerging science of detection; now we are obsessed with the forensic detail of violent death. And no other genre has so captivated and enthralled readers.

Vast troves of classic crime writing have for a long time been unavailable to all but the most dedicated frequenters of second-hand bookshops. The advent of digital publishing means that we are now able to bring you the backlists of a huge range of titles by classic and contemporary crime writers, some of which have been out of print for decades.

From the genteel amateur private eyes of the Golden Age and the femmes fatales of pulp fiction, to the morally ambiguous hard-boiled detectives of mid twentieth-century America and their descendants who walk our twenty-first century streets, The Murder Room has it all. >>>

The Murder Room
Where Criminal Minds Meet

themurderroom.com

Anthony Gilbert (1899–1973)

Anthony Gilbert was the pen name of Lucy Beatrice Malleson. Born in London, she spent all her life there, and her affection for the city is clear from the strong sense of character and place in evidence in her work. She published 69 crime novels, 51 of which featured her best known character, Arthur Crook, a vulgar London lawyer totally (and deliberately) unlike the aristocratic detectives, such as Lord Peter Wimsey, who dominated the mystery field at the time. She also wrote more than 25 radio plays, which were broadcast in Great Britain and overseas. Her thriller *The Woman in Red* (1941) was broadcast in the United States by CBS and made into a film in 1945 under the title *My Name is Julia Ross*. She was an early member of the British Detection Club, which, along with Dorothy L. Sayers, she prevented from disintegrating during World War II. Malleson published her autobiography, *Three-a-Penny*, in 1940, and wrote numerous short stories, which were published in several anthologies and in such periodicals as *Ellery Queen's Mystery Magazine* and *The Saint*. The short story 'You Can't Hang Twice' received a Queens award in 1946. She never married, and evidence of her feminism is elegantly expressed in much of her work.

By Anthony Gilbert

Scott Egerton series
Tragedy at Freyne (1927)
The Murder of Mrs
  Davenport (1928)
Death at Four Corners (1929)
The Mystery of the Open
  Window (1929)
The Night of the Fog (1930)
The Body on the Beam (1932)
The Long Shadow (1932)
The Musical Comedy
  Crime (1933)
An Old Lady Dies (1934)
The Man Who Was Too
  Clever (1935)

Mr Crook Murder
  Mystery series
Murder by Experts (1936)
The Man Who Wasn't
  There (1937)
Murder Has No Tongue (1937)
Treason in My Breast (1938)
The Bell of Death (1939)
Dear Dead Woman (1940)
  aka *Death Takes a Redhead*
The Vanishing Corpse (1941)
  aka *She Vanished in the Dawn*
The Woman in Red (1941)
  aka *The Mystery of the
  Woman in Red*

Death in the Blackout (1942)
  aka *The Case of the Tea-
  Cosy's Aunt*
Something Nasty in the
  Woodshed (1942)
  aka *Mystery in the Woodshed*
The Mouse Who Wouldn't
  Play Ball (1943)
  aka *30 Days to Live*
He Came by Night (1944)
  aka *Death at the Door*
The Scarlet Button (1944)
  aka *Murder Is Cheap*
A Spy for Mr Crook (1944)
The Black Stage (1945)
  aka *Murder Cheats the Bride*
Don't Open the Door (1945)
  aka *Death Lifts the Latch*
Lift Up the Lid (1945)
  aka *The Innocent Bottle*
The Spinster's Secret (1946)
  aka *By Hook or by Crook*
Death in the Wrong Room
  (1947)
Die in the Dark (1947)
  aka *The Missing Widow*
Death Knocks Three Times
  (1949)
Murder Comes Home (1950)
A Nice Cup of Tea (1950)
  aka *The Wrong Body*

Lady-Killer (1951)

Miss Pinnegar Disappears (1952)
  aka *A Case for Mr Crook*

Footsteps Behind Me (1953)
  aka *Black Death*

Snake in the Grass (1954)
  aka *Death Won't Wait*

Is She Dead Too? (1955)
  aka *A Question of Murder*

And Death Came Too (1956)

Riddle of a Lady (1956)

Give Death a Name (1957)

Death Against the Clock (1958)

Death Takes a Wife (1959)
  aka *Death Casts a Long Shadow*

Third Crime Lucky (1959)
  aka *Prelude to Murder*

Out for the Kill (1960)

She Shall Die (1961)
  aka *After the Verdict*

Uncertain Death (1961)

No Dust in the Attic (1962)

Ring for a Noose (1963)

The Fingerprint (1964)

The Voice (1964)
  aka *Knock, Knock! Who's There?*

Passenger to Nowhere (1965)

The Looking Glass Murder (1966)

The Visitor (1967)

Night Encounter (1968)
  aka *Murder Anonymous*

Missing from Her Home (1969)

Death Wears a Mask (1970)
  aka *Mr Crook Lifts the Mask*

Murder is a Waiting Game (1972)

Tenant for the Tomb (1971)

A Nice Little Killing (1974)

Standalone Novels

The Case Against Andrew Fane (1931)

Death in Fancy Dress (1933)

The Man in Button Boots (1934)

Courtier to Death (1936)
  aka *The Dover Train Mystery*

The Clock in the Hatbox (1939)

The Visitor

Anthony Gilbert

An Orion book

Copyright © Lucy Beatrice Malleson 1967

The right of Lucy Beatrice Malleson to be identified as the author of this work
has been asserted in accordance with the Copyright, Designs and Patents Act
1988.

This edition published by
The Orion Publishing Group Ltd
Orion House
5 Upper St Martin's Lane
London WC2H 9EA

An Hachette UK company
A CIP catalogue record for this book is available from the British Library

ISBN 978 1 4719 1030 2

www.orionbooks.co.uk

I was grinding coffee in the electric machine when my flat bell rang. It was only eight-thirty, so it had to be either the postman or Joe to read the electric meter, and as the postman had gone by it would be Joe. He always comes early to catch the workers; he says if he leaves cards only fifty per cent of the people fill them up, and half those fill them up wrong.

Joe never seems to be in a hurry, but this morning the bell rang for the second time before I could reach the door.

"Where's the fire?" I began, flinging it open, and stopped, feeling a fool. Because it wasn't Joe, after all, it was a man I'd never seen before. It was odd, seeing how undistinguished he looked, a bit below normal height, sallow complexion, unemphatic manner, that I knew from that first minute he spelled danger. He wore an off-the-peg Burberry and a soft hat pulled over his face.

"Mrs. Ross?" he said.

"Yes," I told him. "But I don't think I'm the one you want."

"Oh?" he said, sounding barely interested. "Are there two?"

"There's Mrs. Paula Ross at number thirty-four," I told him. "I'm always getting her mail." I found myself hoping desperately she was the Mrs. Ross he wanted.

"The one I'm looking for has a son called Philip at Oxton University."

So it was me—fear poured over me like a bucket of dirty water.

"What's happened to Philip?" I cried. "Is it an accident?" Only, he didn't look like the police.

"You could put it that way." Cool, dispassionate, barely interested you'd say. It did go through my mind that he was the kind who makes an ideal secret agent. Once you've passed him in the street you don't even remember what he looks like.

"Are you the police then?" I had to ask.

"In that case I'd have to declare an interest, wouldn't I?" He sounded as unmoved as the man in Philip's old weather-box, who never came out any more, rain or shine.

"What's happened to my son?" I demanded frantically. The electric kettle was flooding the kitchen with steam.

"Can I come in?" my visitor suggested. All this time old Miss Muir from the ground floor had been loitering in the hall, ostensibly sorting the post. She used to hold up the envelopes to the light; sometimes I wondered if she had second sight and could see through the covers. I thought perhaps that's how people start on blackmail. I didn't guess how much more I was going to learn about the subject during the next quarter of an hour.

I stood back. "I was just making some coffee."

"I wouldn't want to stop you doing that, Mrs. Ross."

He walked into the living room as though he owned it. "This is nice," he said.

Philip and I had decorated it last year. It has one long wall covered with dark green architect's paper and we had spent a whole day mixing paint to get the right mushroom shade for the ceiling. He stood in front of the picture we found in the Portobello Market, a brilliant horizontal panel of fruit and wine bottles on a dark ground. In the darkest day it gathers up any light there is and throws it back onto the air.

I poured the coffee into a paper cup and set it to drip while I found cups and saucers. My visitor, whose name I didn't yet know, went on chatting as though this were just a social call. "When I was a young chap and believed that money would get you anything, I used to dream of a room like this one, it seemed so simple, just choose what you want, get it delivered, but it's a gift, isn't it? I mean, I could buy this place up ten times over and never feel it, but then I couldn't create the room in the first place. Is that him—your son, I mean?"

He crossed the room and took up a photograph of Philip from my writing desk. It occurred to me that this was how bailiffs must behave, making themselves at home, handling your possessions as of right.

"Doesn't favor you much, does he?" He put the frame down. "Takes after his father, perhaps."

I brought the coffee in, poured him a cup.

"Sugar?" he asked. He'd sat down without being invited. So I had to go back to the kitchen and fetch it. Philip and I don't take it, so I forget to put it on the tray. "Annette always liked them dark," he went on as if he were continuing a conversation. "I'm on the fair side myself." He'd removed his hat at last, revealing a lot of thick mouse-colored hair with no more vitality than his general manner. It even looked as though it had been nibbled by mice rather than cut. I wondered who

Annette could be. He didn't look old enough to have a daughter of the right age to interest Philip.

"Who is she?" I asked abruptly.

He handed his cup back. "That was good. I wish I could persuade her to make coffee as good as that. If there is another cup . . ."

I felt that if there hadn't been I should meekly have offered to make a fresh pot. I refilled the cup and passed it back.

"Annette's my wife," he said. "Her and your boy have been having themselves a ball during the vacation —isn't that what they call holidays when you're at a university?—and not just for coffee." He drank his coffee; his eyes were on me like magnets. "News to you? I believe it is. It was news to me once. Oh—I should introduce myself." He put his hand in his pocket and pulled out a business card. Alfred Samson, I read, and an address in Maygate Street, London, W. II.

"Samson!" I repeated incredulously. I almost laughed. It seemed such a silly sort of joke. It was obvious he'd heard it a nauseating number of times.

"Good for a laugh any day of the week, isn't it?" he agreed. "Anyhow, it was when I was at school. Nowadays chaps don't laugh so much." I could believe, too. "No, keep it, Mrs. Ross. I've a feeling you're going to need it." I had the same feeling myself.

"How old's your wife?" I heard myself ask before I knew I was going to speak at all.

"She's twenty-seven, though most people don't believe it."

"Philip won't be twenty for two months," I said sharply. "He's only a boy." Afterward I realized it hadn't occurred to me to doubt his word.

"Chaps younger than him could be hanged up to a year or two ago, they can still fight for their country, get married, get a life sentence, come to that. And it

4

seems they can make love to other men's wives."

"It doesn't seem to have occurred to you that I'm the one with a grievance," I exploded. "A married woman seducing a boy . . ."

"Now, come, Mrs. Ross." I wondered if anything would disturb his surface placidity. "One of these days the girl your boy marries is going to be grateful to Annette. Love's like everything else, there's a right and a wrong way of doing it, and I daresay several in between, and Annette knows them all."

I drained my cup in what I hoped was a casual way, but the clattering of the cup against the saucer as I put it down betrayed me. I was sick with fear and this little rat knew it.

"I still don't understand why you've come to me," I said. But of course there were only two reasons, and one was money. It must have been obvious that any month I broke even was my lucky month, and for all his insignificant bearing he reeked of the stuff. So—if it wasn't money, it had to be revenge. I pulled out my cigarettes and lighted one, but that was a mistake, because I couldn't hold the match steady enough to get it going. Samson leaned across with his lighter. "You say that my son . . ."

"Oh, it's more than saying, Mrs. Ross. He's condemned out of his own mouth, well, pen rather. Even if Annette hadn't admitted it."

That winded me. "You mean there are letters."

"That's what I mean."

"Addressed to your wife?"

He nodded again.

"And you've *read* them?"

"Why not? Husbands and wives are supposed to have everything in common. Mind you, he must have something, this young chap. How old should you say I was?"

I hesitated. "Thirty-seven?" I offered. "Thirty-eight."

It was difficult because he was the type that seems to have been born his present age. I couldn't imagine him a young man any more than I could imagine him old. He gave me a wintry smile, the first of the interview.

"Near enough," he said. "Anyway, it's a long time since I was a young fellow, but reading these letters took me right back to my first girl. She was called Althea, I remember. Funny, I haven't thought of her in years. A redhead, red as a fox, smelled like one, too, the way some redheads will. But exciting. And wily as a vixen. I'd forgotten what it felt like, being young." He stopped a minute, mysteriously lost in the past. "He should have lived in the days when you wrote other chaps' love letters for a fee. Well, it could come to that yet."

"I don't know what you mean."

"He's at Oxton University, didn't you say?"

"You told me, but—yes, it's true."

"I wonder what his professors would think if they read these." He hauled an envelope out of his pocket, from which he extracted a number of documents. "Recognize the writing?"

Well, of course I did. Any mother recognizes her son's hand, even if she doesn't see it often.

"Those aren't letters," I objected.

"Photostats. They'd come to the same thing in a court of law."

Suddenly I felt calmer. "You're bluffing," I told him. "You're not coming into court with a story like that. It may be very unfair, but the husband who's made to wear horns by a boy of nineteen can't expect much sympathy. In fact," I added, my common sense suddenly reeling, "all he usually gets is ridicule. He seems a bit of a joke."

"People have made that mistake about me before," Samson said. "They're none of them laughing now." I felt the first pricks of alarm. My first sense had been one of panic. This was much worse. He wasn't only a danger to me, he was a danger to Philip, too. "And, of course, I don't have a divorce in mind. Annette's my responsibility, even if he has horned in. But I wonder what would happen to his scholastic career if the facts became public."

"You really mean that," I said. "You'd really do that. Wreck his prospects . . ."

"I'm one of the people who work sixteen to eighteen hours a day to make it possible for young chaps like your son to have everything for free," Samson said. "I went to work myself when I was fifteen . . ."

"Why, you're jealous!" I cried. "You can't bear it that he should have privileges that were denied to you. But that's setting your face against progress . . ."

"As I understand it, there are always more young fellows wanting to get into these colleges than there are places for them, and better lads than yours to fill them. All this higher education doesn't seem to have taught him much about meum and tuum. It's not just the letters," he went on, "there's the matter of the check."

"The check?" I repeated. I felt like an anemic parrot.

"The check for a hundred pounds your bright lad forged."

"Who says so?" I demanded. "You can't make charges like that. Anyway, why would he want a hundred pounds?"

"To buy off this chap who had the photograph. Pour yourself some more coffee, Mrs. Ross, and let me do the talking for a bit. If you don't believe my story you can tackle your son. Now, Annette and I have a joint banking account, it's quite customary between husbands and wives."

"You must have a lot of confidence in her," I suggested, "if you don't mind her knowing your business deals."

"Try keeping her out," Samson told me laconically. "She was my secretary before she was my wife. There's more to being a good secretary than being able to write shorthand at two hundred words a minute. She was as smart as a whip and decorative with it. It's funny," he brooded, "how seldom beauty and brains go together."

But that's not why you married her, I reflected. You married her because she knew too much. I could easily believe that where Mr. Samson was concerned there was a good deal to know. Not that I imagined he couldn't draw a check without consulting her. He'd have a second account somewhere, probably in another name.

"What's this about my son and a check?" I demanded.

"They must have been mad to think I wouldn't find out. That is, he was mad, she didn't know till it was too late." (So that's the way she was going to tell it.) "I'm a businessman, I work hard for my money and I like to see value for it. I don't mind spending it, but it's got to show a return, and if that's mercenary, then mercenary is what I am. I go through my monthly statements—I have an arrangement with my bank to send them to me each month—and when I find my wife drawing two checks for a hundred pounds within four days of each other I want to know what's happened to the money. So—knowing I hadn't signed it—I started putting questions."

"And you found . . . ?" My mouth was as dry as a desert.

"I found that one of the checks had been cashed by a young fellow none of the tellers recognized. Mind you, on the surface it all seemed correct enough. Annette's signature and mine just as it should be, if I'd been the clerk in question I'd have accepted it, too. Turned out he was new to the job, no reason for him to suspect any monkey business . . . Only, I wasn't even in town the day the second one was signed."

"So you leaped to the conclusion that my son had forged your signature?"

"No leaping about it. It was a simple matter of elimination. Annette couldn't sign my name in a manner to get past a bank clerk to save her life; anyway, the young fellow admits it."

"You mean, you've *spoken* to Philip?"

"I've spoken to my wife. Oh, there's no doubt about it."

"Did she add that she put him up to it—assuming it's true?" I demanded.

"According to Annette, she knew nothing till I showed her the check, took her by surprise, so she didn't even have time to think up a story. She says she'd never have let him do anything so crazy."

"Does she explain how he managed to lay hands on a check form, one she must have signed, if she knew nothing?"

"My wife's not as careful as I'd like to see her. She has these checks in an open drawer waiting for my signature."

"It's not a very pretty picture you're painting of my son. Rummaging through her drawers. And how did he know your bank signature?"

Samson shrugged. "I daresay he'd seen it on some other check. One thing I will say for Annette, she's never objected to my paying for her luxuries. Tell me, Mrs. Ross, has he ever been in this sort of trouble before?"

I was dumb. I thought if I had a cleaver handy I could find a very good use for it. It had been a family joke, Philip's ability to copy signatures when he was still a schoolboy. A joke, yes, but there'd been a day when he was sixteen when my sister, Susan, got a letter

ANTHONY GILBERT

from a man who hung around but never came up to scratch, proposing marriage in the most violent and poetic terms. She brought it to me. "I don't know what's come over Jim," she said. "Just listen to this. Quoting Chaucer. The only Chaucer he'd ever have heard of would be a race horse." "Perhaps he's trying to adopt a little culture to come up to your standards," I chaffed her. And then I realized she was in a white rage. "Standards nothing! This is one of Philip's jokes. I'm sorry for you, Margaret, really I am, giving birth to a son with all the makings of a criminal . . ." Philip hadn't even denied it. "I thought it was time someone did something about it," he explained reasonably. "Here was Jim, blocking the fairway and keeping out more suitable craft . . ."

Susan never did marry Jim, though I always believed he was the one she wanted. The following year she married another man and it worked out all right; they were killed together in an air crash twelve months later. I've never quite got used to a world without Susan in it, in a way I miss her even more than George, who was my husband for more than thirteen years.

Samson was watching me like a hawk. "Makes a habit of it, does he?"

"Of course not," I said. "And I'd like to hear my son's side of it. What made him stop at a hundred pounds?" I added recklessly.

"I told you, that's the sum this fellow was asking."

"Oh yes—the photograph. Was it worth the money?"

"Annette must have thought so, since she paid it."

Another thought struck me. "Where did she suppose Philip got a hundred pounds from, a boy of nineteen at Oxton on a scholarship, unless she helped him?"

"He told her he got it from his father."

Someone laughed, a hideous raucous sound. "It's not funny," I cried indignantly, and then I saw my com-

10

panion's face. It was as solemn as Good Friday morning.

"Did he add that his father and I were separated six years ago and I got my divorce for desertion when my son was seventeen? He's in New Zealand now, George, I mean."

Samson was shaking his head. "That's not how your lad tells it. According to him he's doing very nicely, thank you, big place in the Lake District."

"I shouldn't think George has ever been in the Lake District in his life."

"So he's a liar as well as a fornicator and a forger. He doesn't believe in half measures, does he?"

"What happened to the photograph?" I said.

"She destroyed it—naturally."

"And was it worth all that money?" I repeated.

"I couldn't say. I never saw it."

"So you've only her word that it existed. Or that Philip was featured in it. I daresay he wasn't the only string to your wife's bow."

Samson's face sharpened and shrank; now he looked like a white rat. "That was a mistake, Mrs. Ross. You're in bad enough trouble as it is."

"There's such a thing as proof," I pointed out. "If Philip denies this, it'll be just your wife's word against his. And I still don't see how he could be sure about your signature."

"He could have seen a letter . . ."

"My son doesn't read other people's letters."

"Why not? He's not above stealing their wives and forging their signatures."

I poured myself more coffee. "Where is it now, this precious check?"

"Where it should be—in my safe—until it's redeemed. And don't think an expert couldn't tell if the signature's faked."

11

"What it amounts to is you claim my son owes you a hundred pounds." I tried to sound disdainful, but I'd no more idea where I could raise such a sum on the spur of the moment than I'd have had of reaching the moon.

"If you were thinking of redeeming it," said Samson in his monotonous voice, "the price is five hundred pounds."

I couldn't believe it. "But that's blackmail! The face value is one hundred pounds."

"I'm a businessman, Mrs. Ross, and I was given to understand you were a businesswoman. You'd be buying in a seller's market. What's this job of yours?"

"I'm a free-lance journalist."

"Writing for this paper and that?"

"Writing for anyone who's in the market for my work."

"And naturally you get the best price you can?"

"Naturally. Though mostly I take what I'm offered."

"And I bet they know it. You'll never be a rich woman that way, Mrs. Ross."

"I'm certainly not one now. It would be hard enough to raise a hundred pounds, five hundred's out of the question."

"You haven't stopped to think. You don't give me the impression you're the sort that's easily defeated. You must have something of value you could sell. How about this flat?"

"I have it on lease, it's got about two years to run. I thought it would just see Philip through Oxton."

"The furniture? You've got some nice pieces."

"There's not much sense having a flat without any furniture."

"Pictures?" He looked round, shaking his head. "No, you've a nice taste, but people don't pay for that. How about your bank?"

"I could hardly ask Mr. Wilson to advance me five

hundred pounds for a blackmailer." You'll see that I'd quite accepted Samson's version of the story. Mind you, I didn't think it was a one-man effort; Annette had known all about the check, most likely the suggestion had come from her. Still, that wouldn't help Philip much now.

"That tongue of yours will get you into trouble yet," he warned me. "Well, then—jewelry?"

I shook my head.

"That brings us back to the boy's father."

"He's in New Zealand, I told you. I don't even know his address. And if I did he wouldn't have the money, and if he had he wouldn't send it."

"His own son?"

Well, I knew George would never accede to a black-mail demand. The thin end of the wedge he'd call it; he might go out looking for Samson, but he wouldn't take his checkbook with him.

"Alimony?" Samson was certainly a trier.

"I never asked for any. Seven years ago I was young and strong and able to work." I don't think the thought of alimony had ever passed through George's head. He'd never seen a husband as a provider. Up till the time of the divorce sums of money were paid into my account toward Philip's education, but not at regular intervals and never the same amount. Then, after the divorce, I heard through his bank that he was going abroad, if I wanted to get in touch I could do it through them, but I'd never tried. George was—presumably is—a likable man; in a way he was the reason I hadn't married again. He'd have no trouble in getting another wife. I remem-bered his last words to me as he walked away as casually as if he were strolling to the corner to post a letter.

"Good-bye, my darling. If you ever get the time you should visit the Natural History Museum and make the acquaintance of the black widow spider. One of the most efficient and methodical of nature's inventions— but she can't keep a husband."

"There's one solution you haven't considered," I told Samson. "I might call your bluff. Refuse to buy."

He shook his head. No amount of shaking stirred that mat of mouse-colored hair; it might have been glued on to his head.

"I'm not bluffing. And you'll come up with something. This boy's all you've got, and his future's in your hands. I appreciate you've had a shock. I think you've taken it very well, the lad's lucky to have you. What you want now is time. How about meeting me tomorrow night, say, at the Queens Hotel near Paddington Station? It's a small impersonal place, people coming and going all the time, waiting for trains, waiting for friends, they'd scarcely recognize royalty. How about five o'clock? That gives you eighteen hours or so to make a plan. Why, you might even find you could bring the money with you."

"Or a lawyer," I said.

"You don't know much about me, do you, Mrs. Ross? But others are different. If your lawyer knows how many beans make five he'll tell you to settle out of court, if your son means anything to you, that is. And don't try and contact my wife . . ."

"I don't even know where I'd find her," I told him contemptuously.

"Under my roof, naturally, where a wife should be. And she won't be seeing your boy again. I have her word for that. I can see what you're thinking, but I promise you she'll keep it. Annette knows which side her bread's buttered, and she doesn't like it dry, any more than anyone else. Had too much of that in her past, savvy? She came up the hard way, too. Well, I

14

mustn't keep you from your work, Mrs. Ross. And
thanks for the coffee. We'll meet again tomorrow."

"I wouldn't count on that," I said, but of course I
knew I should be there. I hadn't any choice.

II

After Samson had gone I sat for a while waiting for the dust to settle. My impulse was to dash around like an exasperated gadfly, start heaving furniture about, turn out my wardrobe, start on the laundry, anything to allay the panic he had aroused. But I just stayed put, and presently I was able to make plans. I've learned something about the need for patience in my work. The temptation to get something, anything, onto paper when I have a tough assignment is often overwhelming, but in my experience it never gets you anywhere. I only exhaust myself and end up more muddled than I started. I have to get my ideas into order, set them on a foundation. That's what I did now.

When I knew my next step I got up, cleared away the cups, which I washed and hung in the kitchen, straightened the cushions and picked up the telephone to ask for telegrams. I sent Philip a wire telling him to call me at the Crown Hotel, Oxton, any time after three P.M. Very urgent, I said. Then I packed an overnight case, counted my cash, thank goodness I'd been to the bank the day before, rang for a taxi and was driven to Euston, the impossible station from which the Oxton trains run. I was always telling myself next time I'd go by Green Line coach and save about ten shillings in fares, but I never did. I didn't today either.

At the station I found I had twenty minutes to wait. I telephoned from a coin box to cancel a lunch engagement, told an agitated female with an ancient mum where to find the loo and then discovered my train was in. Waiting for it to start I tried to imagine my conversation with Philip. I told myself he'd laugh, not with amusement but with indignant disbelief, before I was halfway through, but I knew that was wishful thinking. Men like Alfred Samson don't waste their time, all of it loaded, playing silly practical jokes.

I remembered how remote Philip had seemed during his last vacation. I never expected him to give me a lot of his time. His life belonged to himself. I had wondered if it was a girl—well, naturally—and just hoped it would be one I'd be able to like, though at nineteen he could hardly be serious—but I didn't ask any questions. That much at least I had learned from George. I wondered now how long the affair had been going on and where he'd met a woman like Annette. I couldn't believe it was more than a flash in the pan on either side. A woman of twenty-seven married to Alfred Samson might well want a taste of youth and freshness (but why did she have to pick *my* son?); a boy of Philip's age would be flattered by the attentions of an older woman. But it was against nature that the situation should last. It even occurred to me that he had broken with her already and this was her way of taking her revenge. I wished I knew what she was really like. All that was obvious to my prejudiced mind was that at the first sign of trouble she had bolted back to the security of her husband's house, leaving my son to carry the can.

I knew Philip, I believed, as well as any mother can

hope to know a boy of nineteen, which isn't perhaps very well. He had, I believed, a certain sort of stubborn resolution that he inherited from me, and a lot of charm that came from his father. He was, I believed, the quixotic type, again like his father, who would do the wrong things for the right reason. I remembered once how George had pawned the living-room curtains, not to pay our bills, of which there were plenty, but to enable a man he didn't even know very well to pay a fine. A family man, darling, he'd said. You're a family man, I'd pointed out. But poor Jim hasn't got a wife like you, pleaded George. Anyway, you won't want them— he meant the curtains—till autumn, and you'll have got them out of pawn before then. You, mark you, not I.

Even before Philip got his scholarship, Oxton was one of our places. The hills slope to the skyline that almost meets the sea, and in spring and summer the whole landscape is patched with varicolored fields of grain, like a Hilder painting. When I told Mr. Luker, the manager of the Crown, where we always stayed, the good news about Philip, he said, "That will be nice, Mrs. Ross. We shall see a bit more of you, I hope." I felt sure now that though I hadn't booked accommodation he'd fit me in somewhere just for the one night. My first unpleasant surprise was when I found a stranger at the reception desk, who didn't even bother to check his reservations.

"Sorry, madam," he said in an offhand way. "We're full up. It's always wise to write ahead."

"I only want a room for one night," I snapped. "It's an emergency."

"We haven't a room even for one night," he insisted carelessly.

"Perhaps you could rearrange your bookings . . . I'm an old client. Mr. Luker . . ."

He did look up then, scandalized, affronted. "That would be quite out of the question," he told me.

When I asked to see Mr. Luker, I was told he wasn't available. The young man added impudently, "Even he can't work miracles."

I walked away toward a table in the hall. "I'm expecting a telephone call from my son," I remarked airily over my shoulder. "I'll have to take it down here, unless you've discovered a vacancy for me before three o'clock."

I sat down rather quickly, feeling my legs shaking under me. I must have looked on the point of collapse, because after a minute he sent his junior over to ask if I'd like a glass of water.

"The therapeutic value of water has been greatly exaggerated," I assured the youth. He gave me a scared glance and scuttled back to the desk. A bit later the reception clerk came over in person.

"I'm afraid it's no use your waiting, madam," he said. "Perhaps the Cleveland . . ."

"My son won't be ringing me at the Cleveland," I pointed out. "I gave him this number. In the meantime," I recalled, "I've had no lunch."

He beamed with satisfaction. "I'm afraid lunch is over."

"At five minutes to two?"

"One forty-five is the last time we can allot tables at this time of year. Naturally, in the season . . ."

Sandwiches, then, I supposed. And coffee. He'd have denied me those if he could, but there was a notice up: *Non-Residents Welcome.*

"I'll inquire of the kitchen if there are any left," he said icily.

"I prefer them fresh-cut," I assured him. "And not ham or chicken." I saw from his contained glance that I'd defeated him at last. He murmured something to his underling at the desk and disappeared. A minute later Mr. Luker came striding out. It was like seeing the sun come up on a foggy morning.

"Mrs. Ross!" I might have been the one visitor he was waiting for. "Your telegram must have gone astray. Otherwise, of course, you room would have been ready for you."

"I gathered you had no vacant rooms," I said nastily.

"We keep one or two closed at this time of year," he told me in a cheerful voice. "It won't take long to re-open one. In the meantime, how about some lunch. I'm afraid the dining room's closed—staff problems don't get any easier—but sandwiches—let me see, it's cream cheese and walnut . . ."

"Or asparagus tips," I amplified.

"Coffee?"

"And brandy." I felt I needed that.

Within a few moments the whole atmosphere had changed. A waiter came for my order. Mr. Luker was asking about Philip, who had always been a favorite of his. I thought if he had any idea why I was here, that geniality would vanish. I still cherished an absurd hope that Philip would be able to explain the whole situation away.

My room, number forty-two, was one I'd never had before. It looked over the back, over a series of roofs. Far down, along ribbons of roads, I saw toy cars moving as if by clockwork. A toy policeman patrolled the street. A black cat sat on an orange roof and eyed me steadily. I unpacked, the work of five minutes. I looked at the telephone, but there was no one to ring up. By three o'clock, when no call had come through, I began to build up fantasies. Philip had eloped with Annette, had disappeared, unable to face the disgrace—it even occurred to me we might have passed en route, I traveling to Oxton, he returning to London. At three-twenty I asked the operator to put me through to my own number, in case he was waiting for me in my flat, but there was no reply. About four o'clock steps ran up the stairs, there was a perfunctory tap on the door and my son came in, looking so normal I was instantly indignant.

"They told me you were here," he said. "What an exciting parent you are! What's up, Mum? All I can think of is you're going to get married again."

I felt my blood boil at this gay inconsequence. "You don't do yourself justice," I assured him. "I had a visit this morning from a man called Alfred Samson."

"Oh!" He seemed startled but not alarmed, not shocked, not even abashed. "I didn't think he'd come to you. This is my affair."

"Perhaps it occurred to him that you're a minor."

"I don't see what that has to do with it. Anyway, these laws about ages are all arbitrary . . ."

He looked so like his father—tall and dark, rather pale-complexioned, refusing to be panicked—it was uncanny. "Very well, then. I'm your mother—or had you forgotten?"

"Oh, Mum!" he said. "As if I could. All the same, I don't see why you came."

"You will," I promised him. I felt half-suffocated.

Philip had gone to stand beside the window, staring out. He might almost have been in another sphere. "Have you had tea?" he said. "I'll order it." He picked up the house phone. "Tea for two," I heard him say. "Number forty-two. Yes, jam, scones, the lot."

"Not for me," I protested. Whatever attitude I'd anticipated he would adopt, it certainly hadn't been this cool stance.

"What did Samson tell you?" he asked.

"He told me you'd forged his name on a check. I suppose I might try and get you certified. For God's sake, Philip, say something."

"You aren't giving me much chance," he pointed out. "I'd like to think I could make you understand. There wasn't any other way. It's Samson's own fault, really, for creating the situation in the first place."

"You mean, he threw his wife into your arms?"

He winced at that. I'd seen George wince in precisely the same manner. "I mean, Annette couldn't ask him for the money, any more than I could have asked you, though for a different reason . . ."

"Whose idea was it that you should forge her husband's name?" I demanded brutally. "That's what he says you did. Philip, I don't think you realize for an instant just what it is you've done. If he brings a case in court . . ."

"Oh, he won't do that," my son assured me. "According to Annette, he's quite a figure in his own world, and an action would make him look such a fool."

"Did she tell you what that world was?"

"Oh, business of some kind." Philip was vague. "I can see Samson's got you all worked up, but there are two sides to every situation. You don't know what Annette has had to put up with, poor darling. She was so young when she married him . . ."

"She must have been older than you are now," I pointed out viciously.

Someone knocked on the door. It was the waiter with the tea. Philip took it in, tipped the man and poured out a cup.

"Someone—a man—treated her very badly," he explained warmly in tones that held a note of reverence. "Samson got her on the rebound. He's nearly old enough to be her father."

"Only if he married when he was about twelve," I said. "No, I told you, I don't want anything to eat."

Philip piled jam onto a scone and bit deeply into it. Sin, I thought, sits very lightly on the young. I re-

membered what Samson had said about him—a liar, a
fornicator and a forger. It didn't seem to have impaired
his appetite. It occurred to me he was years older than
he'd been three months ago. I was no longer just his
mother, I was a woman in a state for which he accepted
at least partial responsibilty. I didn't have to show him
tolerance now, it was he who showed it to me—a member of the alien generation. I felt my head spin.

"When you meet Annette," he began.

"Meet her?" I could feel myself rearing up like an
outraged cobra. "There's no question of that. She's
gone back to her husband and promised him she'll break
with you."

"Is that what he told you?"

"He says she knows which side her bread's buttered."

Philip looked disturbed for the first time. "I suppose
she thinks this'll make things easier for me. But she
can't stay there, not now he knows about the check.
Even you must see that, Mother."

Even you! There's children for you. "Why not?" I
inquired insensitively. "He is her husband. I gather
there's no question of a divorce."

"He'd never do anything as generous as that. But
he'll make her pay . . ."

"Not her," I pointed out. "You. He's asking five
hundred pounds for the check, and throwing in the
letters to show you what a big-hearted Arthur he is."

"He's having you on, Mother," Philip told me earnestly. "There aren't any letters."

"Then you're not the only forger in the picture. Because the ones he showed me were certainly in your
handwriting."

I saw at last that I had knocked him for six. Not
that there was any triumph in the situation for me. "It's
not possible," he said in a low tone. "I mean, she swore
she'd destroyed them."

"So they did exist?"

"Of course they existed. Well, I couldn't be with her all the time, could I? I couldn't even ring up very often, and she couldn't ring me at all. Mrs. Tribe—my land-lady—has ears like an elephant, they flap in every direction. Anyhow, that just shows you the kind of man he is."

"He's her husband," I pointed out again. "Another thing you seem to have overlooked is that any money she may have spent on you (and it was obvious she must have done most of the spending) came out of his pocket."

"Her wages," insisted Philip. "She earned every penny she got out of him twice over. That's why I don't really feel badly about the check. It was her money as much as his. She worked with him to earn it."

"In that case it's a pity she didn't ask him for it."

"Oh, Mother, how could she? A man who'd read his wife's letters!"

"Letters from another man. Quite a number of hus-bands would object to their wives' having affairs with a boy of twenty."

"Your generation likes everything so cut and dried, doesn't it?" he said. "A husband—a boy of twenty—you can't generalize like that. It's Annette—Samson—me. I'd have expected you to understand better," he added. "When you found yourself in a situation that became unbearable, you could get out."

I knew what he meant. "We'll leave your father out of this," I said.

"We can't pretend he never existed."

"And while we're on the subject, what made you put him in the Lake District?"

"I had to put him somewhere. If I said he'd gone off to New Zealand and left us behind, it makes him sound such a weak, irresponsible sort of chap."

"He was a weak, irresponsible sort of chap. Oh, a charmer and good-hearted, wouldn't hurt a fly, as they say, only fly-swatting happens to be a communal responsibility and you can't dodge it. Don't get any ideas about him being in trouble or anything of that kind," I added quickly. "It was just that it didn't work out. But if you had any idea that he could lay hands on five hundred pounds . . ."

"No one's going to lay hands on five hundred pounds," my son insisted. "He's bluffing. He has to be. I tell you, he'll never come into court . . ."

"He's not proposing to come into court. His idea is to send the letters and the check to the Master . . ."

For the first time Philip looked really shaken. "Oh no, he couldn't do that. You must have got it wrong, Mother. I mean, what good would that do him? There'd be more sense in asking for the five hundred pounds."

"Have you never heard of revenge? Besides, why should he spare you? You've taken his wife, you've taken his money—" I forced myself to say that. "It may have been for her benefit—Philip, according to her she knew nothing whatever about the check, was absolutely flabbergasted when Samson told her about it—naturally, I don't believe that."

"It's what we agreed to say," said Philip. "If questions were asked, that is."

"I knew she was in this as deep as you. Of course you'd never pull off a thing like that on your own—incidentally, did you see the photograph?"

He shook his head. "Annette wouldn't show it to me. She was afraid her husband might somehow get hold of it."

"So no one saw it but Annette. A good lawyer might suggest it never existed."

"I'm not going to let Annette be subjected to a police court inquiry," said Philip. "She's endured enough. Oh,

Mother, surely you can see we've got to help her. I got her into this mess, I owe it to her . . ."

I couldn't really believe he was saying it, no one could be so naïve. "What had you in mind?" I murmured when I'd got my voice back.

"She's nowhere to go, nothing to live on, he's seen to that. What is she to do?"

"There's one little word, four letters—*work*. Alternatively, she can stay with a husband who's prepared to take her back and support her. She's twenty-seven and apparently not an invalid. You're the one to worry about, not your darling Annette. And don't make any mistake about it. If we don't raise the five hundred pounds, and candidly I don't see how we can and Samson knows it, which is why he put the price so high, all those papers—he's got the letters photostated by the way—will come straight here, and if you think the long-suffering taxpayer is going to pay your expenses in order that you can break up someone else's home life—oh, Philip," I groaned, "can no one make you see any sense?"

Philip had gone sheet-white. "I think you'd better leave this to me, Mother."

"Didn't I remind you you're still a minor? Anything you do is my responsibility, whether you like it or not. And here's another bullet for you to bite on. How did Samson know your name unless she told him? According to him you never signed it on your letters . . ."

"Of course she told him," agreed Philip impatiently. "You've met him, you must see she'd never have a chance. He'd twist her arm, probably quite literally, a great bully like that."

A new thought came to me. "Have you ever set eyes on him?"

He shook his head, more impatient than before. "Just as well for him, I should think."

"He's not a great big bully, he's rather an undersized man who objects to his wife taking a lover who makes him look ridiculous—to put it at its lowest."

"Oh, Mother, do you have to be so literal? What I meant was, he'd force the truth out of her—he'd have his own way of doing it . . ."

The truth? Whose truth? Hers? Philip's? Mine? Who could tell? But I could see I was wasting time and breath arguing with my obdurate son. Not that it stopped me, of course. That sort of consideration never does.

"At least promise me one thing," I said. "Don't try and see her, or get in touch—above all, don't try and see him. I'm meeting him again tomorrow . . ."

"Why?" asked Philip coldly.

"Chiefly to explain that we can't raise the five hundred pounds and see what sort of compromise we can come to—if any."

"I won't have it," said Philip violently. "I won't have you contaminated by him."

I felt a sudden surge of love for him. Mind you, I still felt as if I could cut his head off, but the two feelings aren't necessarily opposed to each other.

"I'm contaminated already as you call it . . . He came to my flat."

"Only a cad would think of such a thing. Still, you're strong, Father always realized that. Your mother can take it, he used to say. Annette's different, she's so vulnerable. Mother, why don't you lie down a bit. I'll tell them to send you up a drink at half past six. You'll see things more clearly when you've calmed down . . ."

"When *I've* calmed down!"

"And I think it might be a good idea if I kept this appointment with Samson tomorrow in your place. He probably thinks he can run rings around you."

"He'd have you tied up in a parcel and put in the rubbish dump in thirty seconds," I said.

"It's not as if you had a husband," Philip went on as though I hadn't spoken. "You didn't think a lot of my father, I know, but I can't believe he'd approve of my leaving everything to you."

"It's exactly what he would approve," I said grimly. "And I don't think it's a good idea for you to add murder to your other crimes. Or give Samson a chance of doing just that thing."

"We'll talk about it at dinner," he said. "You've been wonderful, Mum, but the time comes when you have to let the next generation manage its own affairs. And if you think we've no morals, you're wrong. We have, but they're not necessarily the same code as yours. And if we shock you," he added, crossing to the door, "you make our hair stand on end sometimes, too. I'll tell them to give you that call at six-thirty," he added, and went quietly out.

He went coolly away, leaving me dumfounded. I hardly seemed to know this young man, so considerate, so assured, but detached, indulgent even, certainly not turning to me or any member of my generation in panic. One thing he had convinced me of, he was still in love with this woman. At forty a man has some sense, can put love in its appropriate compartment, but at twenty it's like the sun spreading over the sky, blinding him to everything but its deceitful light. That's how I thought of love these days, nature's booby trap. I found suddenly that my head was splitting. I kicked off my shoes, took off my dress. I thought I might be able to think better lying flat. Actually, I did no thinking at all. The next thing I knew was the house phone ringing to tell me it was half past six and a drink was on its way.

III

Something accomplished, something done has earned a night's repose, wrote the poet, but when I traveled back to London by an early train next morning I felt I'd accomplished precious little. Philip hadn't yielded an inch. His last words to me were: "Now, Mother, don't fuss, leave this to me. You'll see, it'll all work out."

How often I'd heard George say that in his pleasant, easygoing way, and how often, sometimes weeks later, I had to clear up the mess. This time I was going into action right away.

As soon as I reached London, I took a taxi to my bank, and ran into another set of frustrations. A pert young woman told me that Mr. Wilson never saw anyone without an appointment.

"This happens to be an emergency," I assured her.

"I'm afraid he's booked up for the whole day," simpered the young woman, displaying teeth that would have earned her twice her bank salary with a dentifrice advertising firm. "Tomorrow—well, no, that's Saturday." Her manner implied that even an unreasonable female like myself wouldn't expect a bank manager to be available on Saturday.

"I'm afraid tomorrow would be too late," I said. "This isn't just an emergency, it's a crisis."

"Perhaps I . . ." she began, but I quickly quashed that.

"Only if you've access to bank funds." Suddenly I was furiously angry. "You don't seem to appreciate," I stormed, "I lend my money to the bank for their convenience. I consider I deserve a little co-operation in return." I set off in a determined manner for the manager's door.

The young woman ran after me in alarm. "You can't go in there. Mr. Wilson has a client."

"I also am a client," I reminded her.

At that instant the manager's door opened and he came out, accompanied by a short, dark prosperous-looking man to whom any bank would willingly lend £50,000. I slipped past him and was in the room before Mr. Wilson realized what was going on. He looked startled.

"I am Mrs. Ross," I announced as he turned back, "and I wish to negotiate an overdraft."

I substituted overdraft for loan at the eleventh hour. He looked rather feebly at his diary.

"No," I assured him, "you won't find my name there. My crisis has only just arisen. I need five hundred pounds, and I need it at once, this morning, in cash."

I thought I better let him have it, both barrels, right off.

Mr. Wilson rang a bell, and said to his secretary when she came in, "Bring Mrs. Ross's account, please, Miss Martin."

"Your initials, Mrs. Ross?" murmured Miss Martin. Neither of them made the least attempt to pretend to recognize me. I couldn't really blame them. My account isn't the type that warrants many calls on bank managers.

I gave them my first name and my address. "No doubt," said Mr. Wilson, playing safe since appearances are notoriously deceptive, "we hold securities of yours, Mrs. Ross."

"Only what are known as invisible assets," I told him. I thought that rather witty. It didn't evoke the ghost of a smile.

Miss Martin came back. I began to understand how beggars feel, going humbly to the back door, having to be grateful for a bit of bread and dripping when they'd hoped at least to be given the price of a pint. Without a word she planked the record in front of Mr. Wilson.

He began to turn over the pages and shake his head. "I'm afraid we've nothing very reliable here," he said. "Preference shares . . . I couldn't advise the sale of those. They wouldn't fetch what you gave for them. Not our advice in the first instance, I believe."

"I don't want to sell anything," I pointed out clearly. "I simply want to draw five hundred pounds on loan, and I want it right now."

He began to say something about the head office.

"You can't have been listening," I exclaimed. "There's no time to consult the head office, unless you can do it on the phone. In any case, you surely wouldn't want to trouble them over such an insignificant matter."

Mr. Wilson leaned back, putting his fingers together. He was a fat little man with treacle-brown eyes. "I often think our lady clients don't understand the ethics of banking," he began.

I picked up a paperweight, shaped like a salamander, and dropped it with a crash on his desk. He jumped and his hands flew apart. "I would like a simple answer to a simple question," I told him. "I need five hundred pounds. I need it in a hurry. I need it for an absolutely essential purpose. Is your bank prepared to lend it to me?"

"Mrs. Ross," he replied with an earnestness that, if ponderous, was, I believe, quite sincere, "a bank is a commercial undertaking, not a philanthropic society. Many of us wish we could be more philanthropic. But we can't entertain propositions unless they appear to us to be advantageous."

"Be a devil," I encouraged him, "and take a chance."

He began to turn the pages of the record. "I see you have sold out stock from time to time, Mrs. Ross."

"That was to pay my son's school fees. I regarded those payments as an investment."

"And—what school is your son at now?"

"He's at Oxton University. It's really on his account I need the money."

The urbanity began to come back to his manner. "I always understood certain funds could be made available in special circumstances . . ."

"Not circumstances like these," I assured him grimly. "Anyway, they've given him a scholarship. I can hardly ask for more favors."

He closed the statement as one closes, with some relief, a dull novel. "What suggestions have you to make as to the method and rate of repayment?" he inquired.

"Well!" I hadn't really thought about this. "I suppose you charge interest?"

He gave me a pitying glance. "Naturally. Just as we pay interest to depositors."

"Well then—say twenty pounds a month."

"So it would take over two years to wipe off the loan?"

"Don't you think I look good for two more years? I'm only thirty-eight, you know."

"And from your record," he continued firmly, "it's

hard to see how you could find the twenty pounds, plus interest."

I'd thought of that, too. "I might have a windfall," I suggested. "I'd put you at the very head of my list of creditors."

As soon as I'd said that I knew I'd made a mistake. He immediately assumed it was a case of robbing Peter to pay Paul, and from that instant my hopes of raising the money were nil.

"I am afraid business is not conducted on expectation of windfalls," he said. "But perhaps there is some other source you have overlooked."

"You name it," I offered. "I don't own the lease of my flat"—it was only two rooms, anyway, and a cubby-hole where Philip slept when he was at home—"I don't run a car, I've no rich relatives withering on the virgin or any other thorn." (He missed that allusion.) "I've no alimony, I've never felt the need of a diamond tiara or known anyone rich enough to give me one. Any other suggestions thankfully received."

"I can only suggest that you speak to this anonymous creditor and persuade him to grant you an extension of grace," returned Mr. Wilson ponderously.

"Grace is the last thing he'd know anything about." I stood up and he breathed with relief. "Give me a little advice before I go, that at least costs nothing."

"Yes, Mrs. Ross?" But he still sounded apprehensive.

"Would you advise me to try moneylenders?"

He almost laughed. "I can hardly believe you are serious." (I thought what a dull life his wife must have, but perhaps, like Annette, she got her fun on the side. Good luck to her, I thought.) "You would find it a ruinous experience, even if, which is improbable, you could find a firm of moneylenders prepared to risk their capital on such security as you are able to offer."

"It's terrible how no one will take a chance these

days, isn't it?" I said. "Anyway, I don't think I have the time. I need the money by five o'clock."

He held out his hand. "I really do wish I could help you. We talk nowadays as though the welfare state solved all problems, but bank managers could tell a very different story. What clients are apt to overlook is that the money we handle is not our own; we have to render due account."

"You're wasted on a bank," I told him with my most brilliant smile. "The Cabinet could do with a man like you."

The woman whose interview I had poached got angrily to her feet as I came out. She was wearing pearls that would have solved my problem six times over. Her trouble probably was she didn't know what to do with her money, she had so much.

I was surprised to find how late it was. Both the manager and his new client were going to miss their lunch dates; they were the sort that always have them. I got a cup of coffee and a sandwich at a cafeteria, and went back to the flat. There were two or three letters on the late delivery, but nothing to help me in my present predicament. I rang up one or two friends to sound them out. I thought it possible I might be able to persuade Samson to accept less than his original demand, but something in my voice must have warned them I was on the borrow, because they started right off telling me the problems that confronted them. Then the telephone rang and it was a commission, and I was so startled I sat down at my machine and wrote a draft right off the cuff. Not that that was likely to help me much either. I wouldn't be paid for a month and I'd only get about twenty-five pounds anyway. By the time that was done I found it was half past four, and I looked as though I'd come out of a ragbag. I whisked into the dark suit, the respectable low-heeled shoes, and added the mourning brooch I had inherited from Aunt Herminia. I only wanted a sheaf of lilies and they'd have given me a place in the first funeral coach.

It was striking five when I walked into the vestibule of the Queens Hotel, but I needn't have worried, because there was no sign of Samson. I had ordered coffee and poured my first cup before he appeared as suddenly as a genie from a bottle.

"I rang your flat to explain I might be a little late," he told me, taking a chair without waiting for an invitation. "But there was no reply."

"Are you sure you didn't ring to find out if I was keeping the appointment?" I suggested.

He looked surprised. "I never had any doubt about that."

"I'm afraid you've had a wasted trip anyhow," I assured him. "I can't raise the money and it's not for want of trying."

"That's going to be bad luck on your son, isn't it?"

"Do you always demand ransom at pistol-point?" I wondered aloud.

He didn't answer that one. "Since you're here," he said, "may I take it you have alternative suggestions?"

"I shall just have to sit back and call your bluff, won't I?" I told him.

"I repeat, Mrs. Ross, I am not bluffing. Make no mistake about that."

"I can't see what you stand to gain. It won't get you your money back, there'll be a lot of publicity . . ."

The waiter came up to be paid for the coffee. Samson put his hand in his pocket, but not apparently to settle the bill. After a minute, feeling a bit foolish, I opened my own purse. As soon as the man had gone Samson snapped open the locks of his briefcase and drew out a big envelope. It was addressed to The Principal, Oxton College. I didn't have to ask what that contained. Instantly my *sang-froid* melted like a plastic spoon on a hot stove. I even had a crazy notion of snatching it and diving for the door, but he wasn't taking any chances. He put it back in the briefcase, which he then locked.

"You're not giving me much time," I demurred. "I only met you yesterday, and practically everything stops midday Friday. Nobody operates over the weekend."

"You might win something on a horse," he offered. "Some of the hundred-to-one runners do occasionally come first past the post."

"I don't happen to be a gambler," I said.

"Too bad it doesn't run in the family. Very well, Mrs. Ross, you can have till Monday, eight o'clock. Come to Maygate Street, you have my card. I shan't be available till eight o'clock, and if you haven't got the money don't bother to come at all. If you're not there by eight-ten I shall know you can't meet my terms and I shall act accordingly. And don't kid yourself I'm bluffing, that's not my way. And you could find it very expensive."

I could believe that now. "You must be in the business on quite a considerable scale," I taunted him. I wasn't prepared for the instant change in his bearing. If ever I saw murder written on a man's face—there's one I wouldn't care to meet alone on a dark night, I thought.

"I'll be there," I promised quickly, "if only to offer an alternative."

"Such as cutting my throat? Oh yes, I've realized that was in your mind from the start. I'm rather surprised you didn't offer me a cup of coffee laced with arsenic."

"I wouldn't know where to lay hands on the stuff," I said. "Nothing else would deter me."

He gave me a sardonic look. "It's too bad we had to meet like this, Mrs. Ross. I like a woman of spirit. All the same, I can guess why you're a deserted wife. Your sort takes such a lot of living up to."

On the way back I dropped into the Owl Tavern and asked for a double brandy. I felt I needed that. But I didn't really enjoy it. I was the only woman there, and I thought the men gave me odd glances. Perhaps I bore the mark of Cain or something. I swallowed the stuff fast and came out in the dusk. I thought I might just have time to walk home across the park before they locked the gates. Not that I don't know all the weak places in the wire where you can squeeze through. I'll get that money if I have to steal it, I told a startled-looking Chinese goose by the Serpentine. The Chinese goose sheered off. It's that or murdering the man, I reflected. At that stage even I wasn't prepared to go that far.

The odd thing was that if I had been, I had the means tucked away cozily in a shoebox in the flat. Soon after our marriage, when I mistakenly thought I was pregnant, George had rented a cottage only a shade less primitive than a shepherd's hut and installed me there to await my infant—in peace and quiet, he explained with one of his innocent, beaming smiles, while he got on with a job that took him around and about and would often keep him away at night. I never quite discovered what it was, I was always a bit hazy as to the nature of George's jobs. I was only certain of two things, that they'd be legal and unprofitable—but because it was so lonely in our neck of the woods and tramps abounded, my fond husband presented me with a pistol and a box of ammunition.

"Not that you'll ever need to use it, darling," he assured me, "but it'll give you a sense of security." He was a first-class shot himself, probably the most popular member of a darts' team the farmer's wife ever had, and he taught me how to use the thing. Every now and again when the loneliness got me down and I hadn't two ideas to rub against each other, I'd take the pistol into the wilderness he called a garden and practice. For this, of course, I only used blanks. I was so remote from civilization that no one ever paid me the least attention except an aged ram who appeared one day from nowhere and eyed me with a distinctly Bacchic expression. After a while, when I found I wasn't going to have a baby after all, and George found, as he was so often to do during our fourteen or so years together, that he'd been misled about the job, which wasn't in the least what he'd been led to anticipate, I abandoned the shack and found a nasty little suburban flat, and George found himself another equally unsatisfactory position. Here I conceived Philip. All the time I was in the country the only human creature who ever came near me, except my husband, was an itinerant preacher who had escaped from the local asylum; he came to borrow a Bible. I must say I found his company quite stimulating, and I never even remembered I had the pistol. When we came back to what's playfully called civilization I brought it with me, and once or twice, when George was more exasperating than usual, I remembered its existence and understood why it is that whenever there's a domestic murder the police's first suspect is the surviving party.

As soon as I got back that night I opened the drawer and found the shoebox. There it lay, looking so neat and small it was difficult to believe it could put out a life as quickly as you can extinguish a candle-flame. It wasn't loaded, of course, but there was ammunition there. Probably the gun wouldn't even work after so long, considering some of the damp places where we'd lived.

The next morning I collected my small store of jewelry and went around to see a man who had occasionally executed small repairs for me, and who might, I thought, be more sympathetic (by which I meant give me a better price) than a stranger. (All through this nightmare period I made one error of judgment after another.) Mr. Bellamy greeted me very pleasantly until I explained the reason for my visit. Instantly he became as grave as Judgment Day.

"Not a very favorable time to sell, I fear," he said. I was sure that was his standard opening phrase.

I put my goods on the counter—a crescent-shaped diamond brooch, a diamond ring, an emerald stickpin that had belonged to my father, a string of small but very well matched pearls. I also produced my insurance policy.

He paid no attention to that. He looked at the pearls and laid them down. Cultured, he said. He shook his head over the ring, I waited for him to say it was only glass; he by-passed the stickpin altogether. He hesitated over the brooch.

"That's nice," he allowed. "I could offer you, say, ninety pounds for that."

"It's insured for a hundred and fifty," I exclaimed.

In return I got a pitying look. I was getting quite a collection of those these days. But he increased the offer to a hundred pounds.

"I need five hundred," I told him. "What's wrong with the ring?"

"It's a very old-fashioned setting, Mrs. Ross. It would have to be reset, which is quite costly nowadays and—well, I have a number of similar rings, and no great demand for them. All this synthetic jewelry. No, I'm afraid I couldn't make you an offer for yours. I don't say you couldn't find a buyer," he added magnanimously, "but you'd have to let it go for considerably less than even the stone is worth."

"Why shouldn't that apply to the brooch too?" I felt belligerent.

"I'll be frank with you, Mrs. Ross. I wouldn't have

offered to buy that if it weren't that I have a client looking for something of this nature, and she wants it in
a hurry."

"I'll bet she pays more than a hundred pounds," I
said recklessly.

"Well, naturally." Mr. Bellamy looked surprised.
"Unless we turn a profit on every article, we should
soon be out of business. Overhead expenses go on, whatever trade is like. Rent—and rates—"

"We all have to pay rates," I reminded him.

"Unless you are desperately pushed I wouldn't advise
you to part with any of the other pieces," he continued.
"As I said, it's a bad time."

"I know. Jam yesterday and jam tomorrow but never
jam today. Well, I'll accept your offer." At least even
a hundred pounds would be an earnest to the odious
Samson that I was doing my damnedest.

He opened a drawer and started counting notes. "I'd
like singles," I heard myself say, and he looked up
sharply.

"I'm not sure . . ."

"It doesn't matter," I corrected myself, feeling that
I'd made yet another bloomer. "I can always change
them at the bank. Suppose I find I can do without the
hundred pounds after all, and your client finds another
brooch she likes better or changes her mind, could I
buy it back—within a couple of weeks, say?"

"If it's for sale, naturally you can buy it, Mrs. Ross."

"For the same as you're giving me?"

"Madam!" His face assumed a pained expression. "I
am not in business for my health, I buy and sell on a
profit basis. If I fail to make a profit I should ultimately
be forced to close down. My own expenses—these
premises, staff, an accountant, cleaning . . ."

"Message taken," I said quickly. "Anyway, I don't
suppose I should be in a position to buy it back."

At his request I counted the notes, which took a ridiculously long time as they were mostly in ones after all, and then I took my discarded belongings and went into another shop that had a pawn-broking department. Here I offered the ring, the stickpin and the pearls.

A sallow young man looked at them in a supercilious sort of way. "Cultured," he observed, throwing the pearls down.

"Did I say they were anything else?" I demanded. "All the diamonds are genuine, though."

He glanced at the pin. "Chips," he said, "and the stone is of no particular value. What were you thinking of trying to raise?"

"I want a hundred pounds," I said. I thought if I offered two hundred cash, Samson might come to terms.

After some discussion he agreed to lend me eighty pounds; I had to leave my name and address and he asked for some proof of identification. A driving license, he suggested.

"First catch your car!" I told him. However, I'd been prepared for this. It wasn't the first time I'd been into a pawnshop since George and I parted, not the first time before that, come to think of it. I offered him my passport. I always keep one up to date, because it's really no more expensive to go to some cheap place in Spain, say, than some revolting watering place on the South Coast. Well, I thought coming out of the shop, my purse swollen like a pregnant sow, that's the end of the line. There was nothing else I could hope to raise money on—there was an odd consolation in that thought.

Because I couldn't stand the notion of the empty flat and the endless wait until Monday evening, I took myself to the cinema that afternoon. The film showed Laurence Olivier in an absorbing role, and though I had my doubts as to the probability of the plot, it was gripping in the extreme. Anyway, since meeting Samson, my notions of probability had expanded somewhat. I went into one of the Corner Houses for tea, then idled along the Mall and paid a visit to the pelicans in St. James's Park. There was a young one swimming alongside its mother. I wished I could give her a bit of advice about what she was taking on. When I got back another surprise awaited me. My son was sitting patiently outside the door of the flat. No, he explained, he hadn't lost the key, he just hadn't brought it.

"I thought you might like some company for the weekend." He explained. "Besides, I want to know what happened last night."

"There was no need to take so much trouble," I assured him. "Everything's buttoned up."

Philip nodded. "I thought Samson would climb down."

"As low as the man in the moon," I agreed.

"I did think you might telephone," my son continued, "only, of course, Mrs. Tribe is a bit of a snoop, and when she adds two and two they come to about ninety-six. I can stay till Monday midday. I told Holy Joe I'd had a message you were seedy. Mother, you're not seeing that fellow again?"

"Not till Monday night," I said, "when you'll be safely tucked up in Oxton. If you have any ideas about seeing him earlier in the day, you can scuttle them. He won't be available. Not that I'm not glad to see you," I added more graciously.

"I didn't think you should be alone just now," Philip informed me.

"Well, really! Did you think I should put my head in the gas oven?" A new thought struck me. "Philip, you haven't any idea about seeing Annette? Because that would finish everything. She's given her husband her word . . ."

"I told you, I came to see you. And try and make you see sense."

"Stop worrying about me," I begged. "I've got the money."

"What—five hundred pounds?"

"I think he may be prepared to come to terms."

We were inside the flat by now, of course, and Philip was roaming about like something in a cage.

"You'll have Miss Muir up," I warned him. "She's very sensitive to noise."

Philip said something refreshingly outspoken about Miss Muir. Then he came tagging after me into the kitchen and stood playing with a cup till I took it away from him.

"We've only got three of that kind left," I pointed out. "There's a milk bottle if you feel you must break something."

"You can't do it, Mother," he burst forth. "I don't know how you raised the money, but even so—surely you can see it's the thin end of the wedge. You'll never get free. I still say he's bluffing, he's discovered your weak spot . . ."

"It's nice you should have become so knowledgeable all of a sudden," I told him. "Find me my cigarettes, will you? They're in my bag."

He was ages getting them. That was George all over again. Ask him to bring you a glass of water and you'd virtually have to tell him where to find the glass and which tap to use. And yet people went on finding them both irresistible. Oh well, I'd found George pretty irresistible myself at one time. It had been a relief really when he went to New Zealand after the divorce. I mean, he couldn't just come strolling round the corner and expect to take up from where he left off. Nowadays, of course, I've developed some horse sense, but at one time

I wouldn't have known how to shut the door, not with him on the other side of it.

I was surprised to find what a comfort it was to have Philip there that night. We didn't discuss Samson any more and we didn't mention Annette. In my heart I was touched that he should have bothered sufficiently about me to make the journey. At the same time my sense of uneasiness increased. Because I wasn't at all sure what this reversal of our roles implied. I've always believed a parent is responsible for a child, no matter how old they both are—well, so long as he's a minor anyhow—but here was Philip taking the initiative, handling the situation, Philip who was responsible for getting us both into it, who hadn't a legal leg to stand on. He even said, "I'm sure you're smoking too much. It can't be good for you."

"I want a transistor radio," I told him. "It costs fifteen hundred coupons. You have to smoke a lot of cigarettes for that."

On Monday I had an assignment I couldn't miss, and I didn't dare arrange to meet Philip for lunch because my plans were so fluid. When I got back to the flat about four o'clock he'd gone. There was a note on the table.

Have had the offer of a lift and am off. Please scrub tonight's appointment, I have an alternative idea.

I was touched again by that, but it didn't make me change my mind. I'd carried the can for so many years, first for my father, then George, later for Philip, it made a pleasant change to have someone worrying about me. But all the same I went to Maygate Street. I put on a caramel jersey suit, no jewelry, a little hat shaped like a jockey's cap with a peak over the eyes—everyone was wearing them just then. Before I left the flat I pulled open the drawer of my bureau and felt for the shoebox.

44

Before I took off the lid I knew what I was going to find—nothing. And I knew why the box was empty. I raged against my son then, throwing dust in my eyes by the handful. That was why he'd come to London, to get possession of the gun. For an appalled minute I had visions of him storming Samson's bastion in Maygate Street, then I remembered he wouldn't be there in the afternoon, it was a shady bit of London, just about suited to the shady business he contracted there. All the same, I remembered Philip's hunting for my cigarettes, he could easily have seen Samson's card in my bag. But there was no reason to suppose he would try and contact Samson; he'd remembered about the gun and had come to London for the sole purpose of getting it. Still, I reminded myself, he had stayed all Sunday; in fact, he had taken me on a river trip to Margate from Tower Hill. I hadn't done such a thing in years, it did me a power of good. Indeed, for a few hours I almost forgot about Samson.

I told myself not to be a fool, Philip wouldn't make things any worse by threatening Samson, that would bring the whole castle tumbling around everyone's ears. Perhaps he really had been afraid I would take the gun. It surprised me, in a way, that he'd remembered I'd had it. I'd shown it to him when he was about sixteen and we had a rash of burglaries up and down the street where we were then living.

"They'll never come here," I said, "they can see it would be a waste of time. But if they do . . ." And I'd waved it valiantly.

"Oh, Mother, do stop frightening me to death," he said. "And I'm sure we'd both be a lot safer if you'd throw it in the Thames."

I thought it would be quite typical of him to have flung it off London Bridge under the eye of a suspicious policeman or tried leaving it on a bus and been noticed by some nosey parker of a passenger. And then I remembered yesterday's trip to Margate, and I felt one of the reasons he'd suggested it had been because he wanted to lose the pistol somewhere where I could never get hold of it again.

"Ridiculous!" I said aloud. "It's probably thick with rust anyway."

I pushed the empty box to the back of the drawer and hurried off to keep my appointment.

IV

Once again I had let time drift on. I'd no intention of arriving in Maygate Street by taxi, I was taking no chances of being noticed and possibly even identified. Waiting impatiently for the bus that didn't come I began to wonder about this intent of secrecy. Surely I hadn't intended to take the pistol, or even if I took it, to use it. Well, naturally not. I'd do a great deal for Philip, who had no one else to depend on, but I wouldn't become a murderess for his sake. That's what I told myself. When at last the bus came it was crowded, and I had to take a short cut and get a bus from another stop, where I was more fortunate. Somewhere a clock was chiming eight as I hurried down Maygate Street. Rank grass grew under ground-floor windows, and old gas stoves and bicycles had been pushed into basement areas. An aged divan, its stuffing gaping from its side, lay in the gutter. It all made Samson's situation seem more sinister than before. You couldn't imagine any honest business being contracted here.

I almost ran down the street, which appeared empty, though I didn't know how many eyes might be peering from behind tatty lace curtains. I found myself blessing television, which kept people with their eyes fixed slavishly on a dark screen instead of on the street, watching the casual passer-by. The only living thing that took any interest in me was a white cat that came sailing like a little ship out of one of the gardens and walked beside me, tail erect, like some heraldic device. You keep out of trouble as long as you can, I warned it, but it made no difference. It marched solemnly beside me and turned in at the gate of number 37. This looked as sleazy as the rest of the street. The ground floor and basement were occupied by the Golden Hind Travel Agency. I'd never heard of them, and decided that by this time next year probably the only people who remembered their name would be those unfortunates who were trying to recover their deposits. *You want it, we have it,* they shouted from a tattered advertisement in the front window. I wondered how much "it" covered, quite a lot more perhaps than tickets and accommodations. There was an automatic porter device and I rang the middle of three bells. If Samson wanted to play the petty tyrant, here was his chance, and it seemed he did, because nothing happened. I waited a minute and rang again, and turned and stared up and down the street. I felt hideously conspicuous; in my mind I could hear invisible voices saying: So she's in the net, too, wonder what he's got on her. I even visualized the news headlines: MAN FOUND MURDERED IN BAYSWATER—UNKNOWN WOMAN ON STEP.

Something touched my foot and I looked down to find the cat rubbing itself against my stockings. I don't have any of the horror of cats some people have, but I shooed it off just the same. I didn't want someone popping up to accuse me of trying to steal the creature. I tried to crush down the horrid thought that Philip had perhaps stood just where I was standing now, earlier this evening; I reminded myself that he'd got a lift, he had to be back in college tonight; the fact that the gun had disappeared meant nothing sinister. In his new role of protecting his aging parent he probably thought he was doing me a favor. A child came out of a house opposite and started dragging a red and yellow tin engine up and down the pavement, squeaking it horribly. In another minute its mother or elder sister would come out and get a front-line view of me. I turned to ring again and found that the door had clicked gently open. I went in, the cat at my heels, and shut the door softly behind me. A few more travel posters were stuck on the walls; they looked as if they'd been there a long time. I went up a long flight of stairs covered with threadbare carpeting and found a door at the top; he must have left this on the latch, because when I pushed it, it opened and I found myself in a small square hall. There were three doors. One on the left stood a few inches ajar, but it was dark inside; the one next to it looked like a bathroom. The door on the right was closed, but a gold beam, rather faint, shone under the crack.

"Mr. Samson," I called, but he didn't answer. I knew that sort of technique, it's supposed to demoralize your visitor, pretending not to know he's there. When I'd opened the door and found him sitting bowed over an enormous desk at the far end of a long room I wasn't surprised a bit. I'd heard it was part of Mussolini's technique; you make your visitor walk about a quarter of a mile to meet you. It's supposed to sap his self-reliance. I remembered going for a job when I was a girl and being interviewed by a woman who played this trick. When I got to her table she hadn't even lifted her head, just pointed to a chair with a pen. "I'll be with you in a minute," she'd said.

Samson didn't even look up, and I felt my blood boiling through my veins. It showed how little importance he attached to anything I could do. "I'm afraid your bell isn't working very well," I told him clearly. "I had to ring twice."

Even then he didn't look up. "One of these days you'll play this trick once too often," I warned him, "and then you'll find yourself on the receiving end."

The room was only lighted by a single lamp on his desk, all part of the build-up, I decided. Deliberately I pressed a wall switch and a powerful pendant flooded the room with light.

Old houses after dark have a life of their own. Boards creak, doors whisper, open and shut, you could swear you hear footsteps even though you know you're alone, and the feet of ghosts, we are told, make no sound. A more likely explanation is that walls store up memories as bricks can store heat, and that accounts for the stirring and groaning that delight psychic researchers and scare the daylights out of ordinary people like me.

From that first minute when I stood beside him, staring at the blood on the desk—the quantity of the blood unnerved me as much as anything, who would have thought the old man had so much blood in him? (momentarily I couldn't place the quotation)—I expected to hear the door burst open, voices, footsteps, feel a touch on my shoulder. I had the impression that there was movement all about me, that invisible crowds stirred. I couldn't think why nobody spoke, unless, like me, they were temporarily numb. I wished I had the courage to switch off the wall light, only I knew I couldn't face the shadows. I dragged my gaze away from the table and the dreadful thing crouched above it—he'd been quiet in my flat, but this was a different sort of quiet. It was as if he'd fallen into an inviolable sleep—*fell asleep in Jesus,* I'd seen that on gravestones. I realized I was approaching hysteria and pulled up sharply. I compelled myself to turn away, and as I did so I saw the door begin slowly to swing open. Clichés are true, after all, I found. I couldn't have moved to save my life, people said; and I'd thought, fantastic, dramatic, but it was true. I didn't know who was coming through the gradually widening gap, but I couldn't do anything about it. I couldn't even pick up a paperweight as a sort of weapon. *Ducky, ducky, come and be killed.* I just stood there and waited for whatever was coming in to make its attack.

Then a frightful sound rang through the room—someone was laughing on a rusty note that was more terrifying than a scream. For an instant I thought it was the corpse, but of course it wasn't; there was nothing ghostly about it either. I pressed my hands over my mouth and the sounds died away. Through the gap stepped the little white cat, delicate as a fairy. I'd thought I'd closed the door when I came into the room, but either the latch was weak or I hadn't quite engaged it. The cat stood on the floor for a moment, blinking in the light; it had two odd eyes, one blue, one amber. I was fascinated. For a moment it stood there, one paw lifted, its face turned upward in a gesture of inquiry. I'd heard that cats hear sounds inaudible to us through the hairs in their ears, which act as conductors. I wondered what this cat heard as it stood there. Samson's last cry, or the cry of whoever had battered in his head? I thought somehow it was humbling that the animal world can prove itself so much more sensitive than ourselves. Butterflies, I'd been told, can communicate over long distances through their antennae. Bats, too, hear sounds where we imagine we're standing in the heart of silence.

I felt clumsy and inferior as that delicate beautiful

creature came stepping delicately across the carpet to leap up on the desk. Down went her little pink nose, out came her tiny raspberry tongue; there was curiosity there, perhaps, greed, a sort of heartlessness that destroyed my sense of inferiority. "You little cannibal!" I shouted, suddenly coming to life. I picked her up and dropped her onto the floor. She stood up, fawning like a dog and licking her pretty little mouth. Her face wore a beseeching look.

I pushed her away, yet in a sense I was grateful to her because she'd broken through my mood of immobility. The sounds stopped, the invisible crowd melted away, everything was dead quiet, I knew she and I were here alone. I knew what I had to do, and I knew I hadn't much time. I can honestly say that at that moment the thought of ringing up the police didn't go through my mind. I was moved neither by compassion nor by reverence.

I walked around the desk, careful to touch nothing, looking for the envelope, it had to be there, it had to be. There was an immense safe standing behind the desk; I suppose it held the secrets of a score or more of lives. Somehow I couldn't see Samson getting up and turning his back on a visitor while he dug out the requisite papers. No, they had to be somewhere within sight. I walked gingerly around to the back of the desk. One of his hands hung down limply, I compelled myself to push it aside and pull open a drawer. The envelope wasn't there but I did see something that had a horribly familiar look. For one frightful moment I thought it really was identical with the object I'd taken out of the shoe box a day or two before. Only if it had been mine it wouldn't have been left in the drawer. Anyway, Samson hadn't been shot, it had been our old friend, the blunt instrument, though when I looked round I didn't see anything that could have done all that damage. The murderer must have taken it away with him, whatever it was.

Abruptly I pushed the drawer closed. The key fell out of the lock, and automatically I stooped and replaced it. I pulled out another drawer and there it was, the envelope I'd come for. I didn't quite believe it, and I picked it up, half expecting it to dissolve. Then I broke the seal and into my hands came sliding the photostats and a letter with a check attached. For a moment I felt furiously cheated because the original letters weren't there, but then I thought that if he had had them he would certainly have posted those, and he had photostated them because he had found Annette's hidden store. It was even possible she didn't know he had read them.

I shoved the envelope into my capacious bag, there was no way of disposing of it or its contents here. I supposed a cleaner or someone came in in the morning to empty trash baskets and sweep the stairs, though there weren't many evidences of any such activity, but I was taking no chances. As soon as I got home I'd destroy all the evidence. I found I was shaking and my breath was coming in great gusts, as though I'd been running. As I pushed the drawer closed I saw another envelope, smaller than mine, with a number on the outside. Number 27. Another wretched victim, I supposed. The fact that it was in the drawer gave me the idea that this might be the next appointment, only Alfred Samson wouldn't be keeping any more appointments. I wondered what 27 would do when nobody answered the bell. I looked anxiously at the papers on the desk to make sure there was no record of his expected visitors, but I couldn't see one.

On the floor the little cat was sitting, its tail wrapped neatly around its feet; its eyes, one blue, one amber, looked innocently into mine. I felt a kind of revulsion for it. Innocence in that room! I wondered how many hearts would rise like larks to know that Samson was dead, and how little they'd care about the manner of his passing, so long as they themselves were in the clear. I didn't know what police procedure was. Would the files in the safe be opened—how else could the suspects be identified? I stood there in a sort of daze, I seemed to have been there hours, but when I looked at my watch I thought it must have stopped. It was barely a quarter of an hour since I'd pushed the door open and come marching up the stairs.

"It's very odd," I confided to the cat, "that the man who isolates and slays a bacillus may get a peerage, but if the law ever identifies Samson's killer, he'll only get a life sentence." It suddenly seemed horribly humorous. I suppose for those first few minutes I really wasn't quite sane.

Suddenly reason snapped back into place. I had to get out, but fast. If I was right and number twenty-seven was due this evening, he might come at any moment. It wasn't enough to avoid meeting him on the doorstep, I had to avoid being seen at all. I tiptoed over to the window—I don't know why tiptoe except that death has that effect, illogically, since the dead can no longer be disturbed—and tweaked back a corner of the curtain. A car went by with two people in the front seat. If they drove like that much longer there'd be more work for the police, I thought grimly, but perhaps they were only making for the dark end of the street, where they could enjoy themselves without interruption. I let them go by, looking nervously up and down. The child had been taken in, you could hear the alternate rumble and shriek of television sets and record players. I hoped the most absorbing programs in the world were being shown tonight. At the corner where the street became part of a crossroads there was an automatic cigarette machine, and a man was standing there reading the instructions carefully. He took a coin out of his pocket and put it in a slot. I suppose he pulled a handle or whatever you do, but nothing can have happened because he began to thump the machine.

"Oh, get on with it, get on with it," I cried. Any minute now the street might be full of cars with courting couples, a policeman might come by or a car draw up opposite and disgorge a party who'd hang about screaming and laughing until Samson's next appointment arrived. I waited, my heart in my mouth, and after a moment the man went away around the corner. I dropped the curtain—I had to chance his coming back or noticing me if he did—and turned to switch off the wall light. Before doing this I gave a long careful look around to make sure I'd left no clue behind me—I hadn't removed my gloves, so I couldn't have left fingerprints—and at that moment the telephone began to ring.

I looked at it as if it were some strange beast barring my exit, and yet all I had to do was ignore it and walk away down the stairs. Only there's something about a ringing phone that's irresistible. It's like a scream in the street—you may know it's no concern of yours, but whatever you're doing you have to move over to the window and see what's going on. Besides, telephone bells carry quite a distance, someone could remember hearing it ring and noting that there was no reply. I didn't think there was anyone in the flat above me, for all I knew it was as empty as the one below, but there remained the odd chance that some anonymous creature would remember hearing the summons and note the time. It also seemed to me—all these thoughts passed through my mind in a flash as they say pictures of your past race through your memory when you're drowning —that if I could establish an alibi for a few minutes after Samson apparently answered his own call, I might be in the clear if anything went wrong and questions were asked. I couldn't stop to work out the logicality of this, that damned bell went on and on. I moved forward and lifted the receiver from its rest. Before I could open my lips a man's voice started to talk, rushing his words together as though he was afraid Samson would cut him off before he'd had his say.

"Mr. Samson? Please listen. This is urgent. It's number twenty-seven. About tonight's appointment. That delivery I mentioned, it hasn't come, an unforeseeable delay. But if you'll wait just a little longer, just a few days, Mr. Samson, please—it's overdue. You know I'm always punctual . . ." The voice stopped abruptly, the sound of breathing was harsh in my ear. I heard myself make a sound that was purely involuntary. It sounded like the grunting of a pig, but come to think of it, it was just the kind of sound you might expect of Samson in such circumstances. The voice had got its second wind. "Are you there, Mr. Samson? Don't cut me off." There followed a sort of laugh, one of the most blood-chilling sounds I'd ever heard. "You remember the old woman who killed the goose that laid the golden eggs? And after that there were no more eggs, no more eggs . . ."

I couldn't stand any more, I dropped the receiver back into place. It wasn't that I felt unsympathetic, I had a horrible feeling that was the way I had sounded on Friday night at the Queens Hotel, begging for a little more time, a little more time. Cringing, pacifying, would-be jaunty, oh, I'd been all of those. Any man who could reduce a fellow creature to such depths of humiliation deserved to die, I thought. I walked down the room, turned off the light. But at the door I stopped, I ran back, I pulled open the drawer and took the envelope marked 27. There was nothing logical about that, I didn't know who 27 was, he might be a right villain

56

wanted by the police and it would be to everyone's advantage that he was locked up, but I'm not the law and he was wearing my shoes. That was enough for me.

And then a hideous thing happened. As I pushed the drawer shut Samson moved. I know, of course, that it was simply a natural relaxation of the muscles. He can't have been dead long when I arrived, and my jolting of the table was most likely responsible, but the effect was horrific. I waited, shivering with fear, expecting to see that dead hand reach out for the phone. I picked up the receiver, let it dangle. Now if anyone rang they'd get the busy sign. I don't quite know how I expected that to help, but somehow it seemed to increase his presumed lease of life. Just till I get clear, I told the cat who had uncurled itself—I had forgotten it was there—and came to stand at my feet.

I rushed to the door, still clutching the envelope, and let myself out. The cat came with me. I made myself pause an instant, but the silence in the house was the silence of the grave. I couldn't even hear my own breathing, because for that moment I didn't even draw breath. Then I was going down the stairs, with the cat beside me, like a streak of moonlight. It wanted to come with me but I didn't dare risk being seen with it. It was probably quite well known locally, it certainly looked well fed. It miaowed indignantly from the dark hall, but I'd more important things than cats on my mind. I was fortunate in that the street was now empty. I turned in the opposite direction from the one in which I'd come, so that if anyone had noticed me passing and was still at the window they wouldn't see me going back.

At the crossroads near the cigarette machine there was a pay telephone box, and I hesitated, thinking I might put through an anonymous call to the police. "There's been a murder at number thirty-seven." Only how would I know? Well then: "There's some funny business going on in thirty-seven, you'd better investigate." Only I'd be asked questions—why was I suspicious? In the end I did nothing. There might be a prowl car in the neighborhood, picking up the message, and they might come swooping around the corner—it might come, I corrected myself meticulously—and see me, and do a bit of arithmetic. A distraught woman, a telephone booth—I couldn't take the chance. He'd be found in the morning, and it wasn't as though anyone could do anything for him. It was too late for that. Number 27 wasn't coming, and as his was the only envelope I'd seen in the drawer, I didn't think Samson would have an appointment after his.

I turned up Coral Street and dived into the tube station. I felt safer underground. There weren't many people traveling, and those there were mostly in pairs. The police are always deploring the lack of observance of the British public. I heard one say once that the average citizen could sit next to a chimpanzee, and provided it wore clothes, not notice it wasn't a human. You can draw a moral from that, I suppose. I got into a non-smoking carriage, then nobody could ask me for a light—I was surprised how intelligently my mind functioned. I got out a station before the one I normally used in case one of my neighbors was coming home and might hail me. Then I found I couldn't go home and spend the rest of the evening brooding. There was a cinema on the corner, and I saw they were showing the first release of the film I had seen on Saturday. The program was almost over and a small queue had assembled for the final house. I joined this, and when I reached the box office I bought two tickets. A woman going to the cinema alone so late in the evening might attract attention, I thought; there are always a few lone wolves who'll make a pass at anything in skirts, and publicity was the last thing I wanted. I went straight in—most of the others waited for the big picture to end—and fifteen minutes later I was swept out again on a wave of humanity. And still I didn't feel I could go back to the flat. Philip might telephone, and I was in no mood to answer any of his questions. I'd take a sleeping pill tonight, I decided, a thing I hardly ever do, and I knew from experience that things always look better in the morning. I hoped that was true even of murder.

I saw a cruising taxi and hailed it, telling the driver to take me to Chez Tomo, a Spanish restaurant where I often went. You were more likely to get authentic Spanish dishes there nowadays than you were on the Costa Brava, where the delicate British stomach cries out for British food. The driver stared for a moment— that was all right. If he was asked, he could remember a woman taking a taxi about two hundred yards from in front of a cinema.

"Do hurry," I said pettishly, "I'm late and you know what husbands are."

He slammed down his flag and a few minutes later we reached the restaurant. Tomo was on the ground floor and recognized me as I came in. I must have looked fairly normal, because he greeted me as usual, he even asked after Philip—people always do—and he recommended the *plat du jour*. I asked for a drink and settled down to enjoy my food, which, oddly enough, I did. For one thing, I wouldn't have dared play with it, not under Tomo's eagle eye. He reacts violently to people who don't appreciate his cooking, and to my amazement I found I was really enjoying it. I hadn't realized how hungry I was and how little food I'd had that day. Tomo came over and talked. People who don't live in London assume its a mighty wilderness of teeming grains of sand, but nothing could be less true. It's a collection of villages. It's true you may not be recognized in the next village, but in your own you're greeted on all hands, even by people who don't know your name. If you're a dog-owner you're known as the dachsie from 19 or the Alsatian from 26; even if you don't have that distinction, you're still recognized. Tomo hoped I had good news of Philip. I said I'd recently returned from a day at Oxton. As the waiter came to collect my plate, my handbag slid to the floor and Tomo himself stooped to pick it up.

Then his face changed. "Señora!" he said, and my heart gave a leap of pure apprehension. I saw his eyes were on my skirt, and there was a mark there as definite as a Sherlock Holmes clue. A child could have told it was blood. "You have had an accident?" Tomo asked. Well, I couldn't pretend I'd cut my finger or anything simple like that because the mark had clearly been made by some small animal putting a bloodstained paw on my caramel-colored skirt. I remembered that infernal cat fawning on me beside Samson's desk. It had already got its foot dabbled in blood. If I'd gone home I'd have seen it, and Tomo wouldn't, and I could have removed the stain without anyone being the wiser. I didn't know how I'd missed it in the tube, I suppose my senses were in too much of a whirl to notice details.

"That wretched cat outside the cinema!" I exclaimed. "I don't know why it jumped up at me, perhaps it was hungry. Never tell me black cats are lucky. Poor thing, it must have cut its foot." I was amazed to hear how natural my voice sounded. "Or perhaps it belonged to a local butcher," I amplified. "Still, not to worry, cold water will get that out." I set my bag firmly on my knee. Someone else came in and Tomo went to greet them. I didn't think he'd give the matter another thought, and even if he did I was pretty well covered.

I lingered over my coffee and as soon as I got back home I peeled off the skirt and sponged it. I couldn't get the mark right out, so I decided to take it, with a couple of jumpers and a short coat, next morning to the Do-It-Yourself-Cleaners who were installed recently at the top of the road. At last, I thought, I'm alone, I can get rid of my damning evidence. In the cinema I had sat with my hand on the clasp of my bag in case it opened and the envelope slid out. I'd put my table napkin over it at Chez Tomo. I had no coal fire here, I couldn't burn the photostats, and anyway I had heard that experts can put even ashes together and make sense of them. I began to cut the pages into small scraps. I thought of flushing them down the lavatory, but I was afraid they might choke the pipe. Eventually, having minced them up, I put them in the one place in my flat where I didn't think anyone would ever look for them. On one of his continental travels Philip had brought me back a big leather pouffe. It was quite flat when he gave it to me, and I had looked at it in some dismay. "How on earth am I supposed to stuff that?" I'd asked him.

"You do it with paper, Mum," Philip had told me blithely. "Goodness knows you have enough from drafts and advertisements and old manuscripts. Cut them very small, though, and pack them tight, or the stool won't be comfortable." I don't know if you've ever tried packing a large pouffe with torn-up paper. Tearing it didn't prove very successful, I couldn't get the stuff small enough; crumpling it didn't pack it sufficiently tight. Eventually I cut—and cut—I raised blisters on my hands with those scissors. Still, when it was finished it did look rather fine. I'd packed it by means of a zipper in the bottom of the pouffe, and then cut a round of thick cardboard and wedged it into place.

Now I got some sheets of newspaper, unzipped the zipper, removed the cardboard and took out the stuffing in handfuls. I spent about half an hour mixing the scraps of photostats with the rest of the rubbish, then I packed it back. It took much longer than I'd anticipated, and I got so exhausted I had to get up in the middle and mix myself a brandy and soda. The envelope marked 27 was another matter. I couldn't put that there, in whole or in pieces, because it didn't belong to me, and sooner or later I intended to return it to its owner. There must, I argued, be some sign of identification to make it dangerous at all. Eventually I put it into a larger envelope, which I sealed, writing my own name on the outside. In the morning I'd deposit it at the bank. Whenever I go abroad I leave—used to leave, rather—my brooch, ring and pearls with my bank. They never want to know the nature of the deposit, and all you have to do when you get back is pick it up and sign a receipt. There couldn't be a safer place in the country—so long as I didn't get myself knocked down by a bus or something, and that's a chance I—and number 27—would have to take. I'd just written my name when the phone rang.

"Where on earth have you been all the evening?" demanded Philip's voice.

"Home for the last hour," I told him tartly. "Before that I was at the pictures." I hurried on before he could ask me what I'd seen; he's an ardent film fan and might remember my going to the same film on Saturday. "And then I had some dinner at Tomo. Nice of you to ring," I added. "I'm never sure with these pickups of yours that you'll arrive in one piece."

"Lucky to have arrived at all," my son assured me. "Talk of going to Birmingham by way of Beachy Head. We must have cruised round a couple of counties. He was a screwball all right."

Instantly I was apprehensive. It's not like my son to offer explanations for anything until you press him like a crushed lemon. Was he conceivably trying to establish an alibi?

"I've no time to play games about G. K. Chesterton at this hour of the night," I snapped. "Philip, where is it?"

"Where's what?"

"I told you, I've no time to play games. Where did you put it?"

"It's quite safe, Mum," he said in a soothing voice. "You didn't want it anyway, did you? Mother, did you go and see that chap?"

"I was doing the questioning," I said. "Who is this man who gave you a lift half round England?"

Philip's laugh came perfectly naturally over the phone. It was that laugh, more than twenty years earlier, that made me think it might be rather fun being Mrs. George Ross.

"Just fancy!" he said. "I never asked."

"And you haven't answered my other question, either."

"I never did approve of you having it on the premises," Philip told me. "I know you always said you'd never use it, but you're so impulsive. Look at the way you threw Father out."

This was carrying the war into the enemy's country with a vengeance. "I did what?" I gasped. "Anyway, he doesn't come into this."

"He came into it twenty years ago when I was born. I never could understand—I mean after nearly fourteen years—as if he was some old hat you'd got tired of."

I heard myself giggle—most inappropriately. "Any woman would be justified getting tired of a hat after so many years."

"I wish you hadn't gone," he said abruptly.

"I suppose you have a better plan."

"Yes. That's why I tried to get you earlier. I must

just have missed you. I had to hang about waiting for a phone, I couldn't call from my digs, the old girl has an extra ear on every wall. I'm in the Blue Pigeon now, it's just closing. Mother, I'm going to the police first thing in the morning."

"You're what?" I nearly dropped the receiver.

"It's quite all right, I shall get protection. I shall tell them I'm being blackmailed—I want you to stay right out of this—I shall tell them everything, the check, the lot. Oh, Mother, don't argue, you must see it's the best way for all of us, for you and for Annette. If we can't pay his demands he'll make her settle, and I can't stand the thought of what he might do. My mind's made up . . ."

Something in my head burst like a great bubble. "Then you can just unmake it," I shouted. "And you can stop worrying about Samson. He won't take any more steps against you or Annette or anyone at all. Samson's dead."

And I hung up on him.

V

After that I didn't expect to sleep a wink in spite of
the sleeping pill, but nature must have known better
because the next time I consciously opened my eyes it
was almost nine o'clock. I leaped up and went downstairs to collect my newspaper. I didn't suppose there
would be anything about Samson in it as yet, but nothing
is ever one hundred per cent certain. In the hall I found
Miss Muir in her usual morning deshabille, a plastic
short-sleeved pinafore over her underwear, a broad rib-
bon holding back her wispy locks. She was reading my
paper so absorbedly she didn't even hear me. She didn't
subscribe to a morning paper herself. What, she asked,
were public libraries for? When she recognized my presence she looked up and her face was a mask of indigna-
tion.

"These people who have no consideration for animals!" she exploded. "Nothing is too bad for them."

"Is that my paper?" I asked as pleasantly as I could.
She didn't seem to hear me. "That poor cat!"

I thought I had enough trouble on my plate without
being loaded with someone else's cat.

"They have nine lives," I reminded her consolingly.

"It's enough to give it a permanent neurosis," she swept on in the same wild accusing voice. "Shut up all night with a corpse."

Whatever I'd anticipated it hadn't been that, but even then it didn't at once occur to me that the corpse might be Alfred Samson's. "Whose corpse?" I heard myself ask involuntarily.

Miss Muir looked impatient. "What does it matter? The man's dead. It's the cat I'm concerned with. The police said when they broke into the house they could hear it mewing like a foghorn."

"I expect it's all in the paper," I offered, putting out my hand.

"Dare to open your mouth and they tell you it's lack of imagination," the old girl ramped on. "What I want to know is, what's the use of all this expensive education if it doesn't teach people to put themselves in the place of the weaker vessel?"

I looked at her respectfully. I couldn't think of anyone else who could have used such an expression. "What happened to the cat?" I inquired. My own nerves were twanging like fiddle strings. Unless she wore ear plugs first thing in the morning I couldn't imagine why Miss Muir didn't hear them.

"Left in a pitch-dark hall with a murdered body on the floor above. It's a pity cats can't talk, it might be able to tell them what happened. Mind you"—here I did manage to tweak my paper out of her grasp—"I always say a lot of the people who get murdered ask for it. The neighborhood alone tells a story."

I heard myself ask weakly, "What neighborhood?" and she answered, "One of those disreputable streets in the Bayswater area. Hotbeds of vice, I wouldn't be surprised. I suppose one should be grateful they didn't batter the cat to death, too."

By this time I thought I realized what she was talking about, but nothing had quite prepared me for what I was going to read when I got back to my flat. The *Record* has the reputation not merely of printing a story in full before most of its competitors, but sometimes of printing it before it's actually happened.

NIGHT CLUB PROPRIETOR FOUND MURDERED
The Clue of the Crying Cat

Mr. Alfred Samson, 44, of Virginia Water and Rush Street, N. I., was found dead in a flat in Maygate Street, W., shortly after midnight. Police broke into the house through a balcony window when all attempts to reach Mr. Samson by telephone had failed. Deceased had suffered severe injuries to the skull. The case is being treated as one of murder. Full story page 4.

Well, you can't say fairer than that, I thought. Even an enterprising scoundrel like Samson couldn't have been responsible for his own injuries. I turned to page 4.

It seemed that the dead man was the proprietor of one of those gambling clubs that have mushroomed every-where in big cities since their existence was made legal by act of Parliament. I had a strong suspicion that it had been working underground for quite a time before that. His club, which was called the Glass Diamond, went the full limits of the law. It catered to all tastes. There was the casino side for those who liked to liven up a dull existence by risking (and probably losing) their shirts at the day's end. There was a blue comedian—and the bluer he was the better salary he could command—to cheer up the tired businessman and there were strippers for those who preferred the personal touch. Even knowing the little I did about Samson I felt pretty certain he kept within the limits of the law in his public life, you could do quite a lot without infringing them. Last night a man who had been drinking and dicing equally reck-lessly had suddenly sprung up and yelled that the croupier had been bought. He slammed his fist on the table, threatened the club with the police and in general created a disturbance. I had done an article on these clubs soon after they came into the open, and I knew that the dishonest croupier is one of their occupational risks. These men know these clubs come and go like swallows, here today and submerged by next week, and if they get a chance of turning a brisk if not dishonest buck, some of them are going to fall by the way. Some of the clubs kept spies in mufti moving constantly around the premises, but they had to change their identities pretty often to avert suspicion.

The fracas—which was one of the *Record*'s favorite words—started soon after midnight. As a rule Samson put in an appearance about eleven o'clock; nothing was likely to hot up before then. But last night he hadn't put in an appearance at all. His manager, Harry Markby, rang Maygate Street but got the busy signal. He waited a few minutes and rang again. Meanwhile the situation at the Glass Diamond deteriorated rapidly. From innu-endo this man, who gave his name as Smith and I sup-pose it's barely possible that it was, passed to outright accusation, sowing seeds of scandal against all and sundry, including the absent proprietor. Violence set in, a table was overturned, a bottle was smashed, some-one got a cut on the forehead. By this time the trouble had spread beyond the casino, and guests were alerted in the other departments. A number of them quietly oiled off before the police came in; the croupiers were madly trying to collect the winnings before these too disappeared. Voices were raised, someone switched off the lights. A woman screamed that she had felt a hand at her throat, whether for murderous purposes or be-cause she was wearing a diamond and sapphire necklace wasn't altogether clear. An anonymous person, who didn't return to the scene, slipped away and called the police from a phone box. Whoever was at the bottom of all this didn't believe in doing things by halves. The word murder was used more than once.

Of course, the *Record* reveled in all this. By the time the police arrived a number of guests had vanished and others were only stopped by the newcomers. Someone got the lights going again. Markby told a police sergeant that he was afraid on Samson's account. He knew the man had been in Maygate Street earlier that evening because he'd spoken to him on the phone. They'd made several attempts to establish contact but (naturally) without result. As a matter of form they got in touch with his West End flat but he wasn't there either. He could have blacked out or had a fall—at that stage no one suggested anything more sinister.

So one of the police cars went around to investigate. Naturally its arrival was a signal for a general reawakening of the street. Lights flashed on, curtains were drawn back. The police rang the bell, then thundered on the door. One of them stooped down and looked through the letter box. There's a cat there, he reported, mewing its head off. They called the man next door, he said promptly he knew nothing, he and his wife kept themselves to themselves, anyway they'd been out that evening celebrating her birthday and hadn't long been back. They knew the man next door had visitors sometimes of an evening but it was no concern of theirs. They'd never seen milk or newspapers on the step, and once when two letters had been misdelivered and he'd taken them in, no one had answered the bell. The travel agency had been closed down for some time, and it never seemed to have been a very active concern. Not surprising, he said. Who'd come to Maygate Street when you can get the same service in Mayfair. A communal balcony ran along the back of the terrace of houses, and the police got into number 37 by climbing a low iron rail and smashing through a window. When they had admitted their colleagues by the front door the white cat came pattering up with them and immediately jumped on the desk.

"You know what to look for," one of the men observed. "Pity you can't talk." It was Miss Muir all 'over again. But, in fact, it talked better than you might have expected, because one of the constables noticed it had a bloodstained paw, yet apparently had no injury. By the time the photographers and fingerprint men arrived the street was seething with excitement. Well, I suppose even a rundown neighborhood like Maygate Street doesn't get a murder every night of the week.

The safe, opened by a key found in the dead man's pocket, was found to contain a number of documents, many of them numbered, and a cash box about half full of notes. There wasn't much sign of a struggle in the room, and the assailant must have entered and left in the usual way. None of the neighbors could help, no one had heard anything unusual or noticed anyone going in or out of the house. But it was the sort of street where your neighbor's business is his own affair. I drew a deep breath of relief at that. No one had seen a woman, accompained by a white cat, turn in at the gate about eight o'clock. I had a momentary pang at the thought of the child, but children are absorbed in their own affairs, and by the time he was collected by his mother or big sister I was no longer on the step. All the same, the bit about the cat's foot shook me. I was remembering that moment at Tomo's when he discovered the mark of a bloody claw on my skirt, but he might not link up the two things, and in any case he wouldn't want to be involved in a murder. Besides, I didn't think he'd imagine I could be in any way connected with a man like Samson. The report ended with a note that the dead man was married and had no family.

No, my chief source of danger was my son. Philip is like George, no finesse at all. If he should be questioned, he'd burst out with the whole story, the police would prosecute inquiries, they'd find out about Mr. Wilson, Mr. Bellamy and the snooty young man at the pawn-broker's. They might even learn that for years I had had a pistol on the premises—though it was a long time since I'd renewed the license—and that I had it no longer. Still, I didn't think even the police would suggest that those injuries could have been inflicted with my little gun. More like a brick, I thought—or a cudgel—and I knew they wouldn't find either of those on the premises. I only hoped Philip had an alibi that would stand up to police questioning, then reminded myself he must have been miles away at the time. And would Samson have admitted him?

At this stage I had such a shock that I nearly heeled over. After I left Samson's room I had had an uneasy feeling there was something I'd overlooked, though I couldn't think what it was, and that sense of unease had followed me all the evening. Now I knew what it was. Samson was dead when I arrived at number 37, there could be no doubt whatever about that. *But I had rung the bell and someone had opened the door.* I remem-bered that other door standing ajar and leading to a darkened room. In my folly it hadn't occurred to me that a darkened room isn't necessarily uninhabited. Someone had known I was coming, had depressed the latch that let me in, had watched—I was sure of it—as I turned to Samson's room. It hadn't all been imagination, the creaks, the footsteps, the mysterious sounds. Some-one knew I had been there, someone who would probably recognize me again. I thought I'd been so clever collecting the letters, destroying them, tearing up the check and flushing away the scraps. Now, I had thought, no one will ever know. But someone—besides Philip, I mean—must know. I'd simply changed one blackmailing tyrant for another, and in a sense I was worse off because I had no notion who the identity of the second man might be.

The next time I saw Miss Muir she was bubbling over with interest about the murder, but I brushed her off. I couldn't hear a step without anticipating the arrival of the police; if the phone rang I thought it might be my unknown witness. *Hullo!* The voice almost took on body in my quiet, too-quiet, room: Is that you, *Mrs. Ross? Just to remind you I know where you were at eight o'clock on Monday night. I'll keep in touch, shall I?* and then the receiver would be hung up. If only I'd kept my wits about me and realized the situation earlier, I could have spiked his guns by getting in touch with the police myself, but now it was too late. Now I had to stand by and see how the situation developed.

For the next day and night nothing happened. Even Philip didn't ring, and I didn't ring him. Whenever the bell pealed I could feel my hand shake as I lifted the receiver, but it was either a wrong number or someone quite harmless. When the front door bell rang I peeped out of my window before answering. I felt like a man on the run. I wondered how long it was before their nerves gave way, I didn't think mine would last long.

When I did get a visitor it was the last one I'd anticipated. When I heard the bell I peeped out but there was no one on the step. Miss Muir was going down carrying an enormous straw basket.

"I've sent your visitor up," she called gaily. "You're a dark horse."

And so I opened the door, and there she was. I never had any doubt of her identity, but she was so different from anything I had anticipated I just stood there gaping. When I thought about Annette I visualized someone small, neat, trim as a bird, with a bird's predatory black eye, round and darting. I couldn't have been more wrong. There's a canvas in the Uffizi by Jacopo, called, I think, "Child with Guitar." It has never seemed like a child to me, more like a cherub, lambent-haired, ardent, and so vital you wait for the lips to open. And here was that child in the flesh, standing facing me and saying in a soft, almost an apologetic, tone, "You're Mrs. Ross, aren't you? Pip's mother?"

I felt ruffled; I detest diminutives. We've never called Philip by anything but his full name. But there was something about Annette that was disarming even to me. You couldn't see her as a wicked woman seducing a nineteen-year-old boy, she looked more in need of protection than he.

"The old lady in the hall told me to come up," said the soft voice. "I'm Annette. I expect you guessed. Is he here—Pip, I mean?"

"My son's name is Philip," I said, "and of course he's not here. He's at Oxton, as you'd expect."

She nodded. "Oh, I'm glad."

I stood back. "You'd better come in," I told her. We couldn't carry on our sort of conversation on the threshold of my flat.

"Why should you think he'd be here?"

"I just wondered," she said meekly.

"You haven't been trying to get in touch at Oxton?" I demanded apprehensively.

"Oh no. What a nice room this is. No, of course not. I promised Alfred, you see." She walked across and picked up Philip's photograph. "It doesn't do him

73

justice, does it? I expect you wish I were at the bottom of the sea."

"I don't know what good you'd do me there," I said.

"Have the police been here?" she went on, standing in the middle of the room.

"They have not," I told her. "Is there any reason why they should?"

She looked at me mournfully. "You're bound to think of me as an enemy, I know, but I only want to help."

"The only help you can give us now," I assured her briskly, "is to stay out of the picture."

She looked startled. "But how can I? I mean, I'm right in the middle of it."

"Of course," I said, "they've been to see you. What did you tell them about Philip?"

Her face wore an air of almost insupportable grief. "I never mentioned him, of course. I mean, they didn't ask me. But—that's what's so awful, being in the dark. I had to know if they'd come to you."

"And now you know—they haven't."

"They could," she said. "If you haven't had much to do with them, and I don't suppose you have, you don't know what they're like. When you think they must be finished they start all over again from a different angle. I thought I must warn you—that I haven't said a word, I mean."

"Why did you come to me?" I asked.

"I knew Alfred had found out, and he said Philip was a minor, and there were the letters."

"It's a pity you didn't destroy those as you promised," I told her bitterly.

"Oh, but I did, I did. It was the most awful thing I ever had to do, you don't know what they meant to me. I'd never had letters like that from anyone in my whole life. Not even Simon." She paused. "Simon was someone I thought I was going to marry before I married Alfred."

74

I had a shocking sensation that any minute now I was going to tell her to put her feet up and I'd make her a cup of tea. I could quite believe Philip had had no idea of her age when they met. To a young man she wouldn't seem much older than himself.

"About the letters," I suggested.

"Alfred's always been an early riser. He must have met the postman, and opened the envelopes. You can do it by steaming them."

"Isn't it obvious when they're opened the next time?"

"I never used to think of that, I just used to tear them open. He can't have got hold of them after I read them, because I never kept them long enough. I used to try and get them by heart—I still can't think how Alfred found out."

If you looked like that after getting one of Philip's letters I'm hardly surprised, I thought.

"Don't stand about," I told her. "Sit down, I was just going to make some coffee."

She surprised me by asking if I had any brandy. I fetched her some and started the coffee to drip.

"Well, you must have realized your husband would notice your getting letters so frequently in a strange hand," I urged. "Unless, of course, he didn't use your address?"

"Oh, he didn't write on the envelopes," she assured me. "I used to enclose one when I wrote back, an ordinary commercial envelope with a typewritten address. And he used to see to it the postmarks weren't always the same. No, there must have been something —I think he had someone spying on us," she added simply.

I reminded myself this was my son we were talking about. I felt sick. "Why should you think—or was Philip one of a succession . . . ?"

She pulled out a cigarette case and lighted a horrible

little cigarette with a ruby tip. "There was never anyone like Philip. Not even Simon. That's what's so awful, that I may have given Philip away. I felt so happy, I daresay it showed. It didn't last long, you know, I knew it couldn't; but you don't refuse food and shelter because you know the time's coming when you aren't going to be able to get either."

"That photograph!" I exclaimed. I caught her by the arm.

"Oh, please," she whispered. "You're hurting. I shall be black and blue by morning. I bruise so easily. I used to tell Alfred I could get a divorce for cruelty—of course, it was all a sort of joke," she added lamely.

"He wasn't contemplating divorce," I said.

"Oh no, he'd never have agreed. It would have made him look—silly—to his business associates, I mean, and his business came first with him. But, of course, if he had a hold over me . . ."

"Which brings us back to the photograph." I heard the water bubbling in the kitchen and went to see what was happening.

"I don't know," said Annette frankly. "That's the truth. I don't know. Only—why should anyone else know about us? You know, I can't bear to think he read those letters . . ."

"Oh, you mustn't think he was unappreciative," I assured her. "He told me they brought back his lost youth."

She looked at me in amazement. "Alfred said that? How extraordinary! I mean, he was the most forward-looking man you could imagine. He said only fools looked over their shoulders, it was a certain way of tripping yourself up. You know, it's funny, I can't imagine Alfred as a young man. That's one of the reasons I married him, the contrast, you know. And then in a way I was sorry for him—I mean, he had everything at second hand. I don't suppose he ever had a real love affair, so he turned to money and power. It was the power he loved even more than the money. He loved to feel I couldn't get away, or if I did he'd ruin the man I went with—that was a stronger feeling with him than anything he felt for me."

I brought in the coffee and gave her a cup. "What made you marry him?" I asked.

"There was Simon, you see. I'd practically bought my wedding dress, everything was arranged, and then he told me he was marrying somebody else. I felt as if someone had put out both my eyes. I was in the dark. And there was Alfred. I had a job as his secretary. I wasn't very good, I wouldn't have been a good secretary to anyone at that time. One day he said it was dishonest to take money you didn't earn, and I said who was I to have the monopoly of honesty, and I could get another job. And he said he was offering me another job, and that's how he proposed.

"It's a funny thing," she said as she sipped her coffee. "I'd always wanted to go on the stage. I suppose most girls do, but I started too late, and anyway I mightn't have been much good. But the first time I really had a chance to act was after I married Alfred. I did mean to keep my side of the bargain. I mean, he knew I wasn't in love with him, but I meant to make him a good wife. And I suppose in a way my vanity was flattered. I mean, a man as rich as Alfred could marry practically anyone. And everybody was being so sorry for me. I couldn't bear it. And I thought well, I might have a baby, that would be nice, because I soon realized I wasn't going to see very much of Alfred. He was busy morning, noon and night. Oh, he wasn't mean, don't think that. And of course any girl loves nice clothes, but you don't want to be just a piece of decoration—put on that diamond bracelet, that'll knock 'em for six—go to Henriques, get yourself a new dress—I was just his trademark, Mrs. Ross, someone to do him credit. When I met Pip he turned me into a person again."

It was a shocking dilemma for me. Here was the woman who'd done all she knew to wreck my son's life and I couldn't hate her. I made my voice very stiff and disapproving. "You haven't told me yet where you did meet him."

"It was at a party. I wasn't at Virgina Water then. I'd been ill, and I couldn't stand the thought of a convalescent home, I didn't need that anyway, but—you don't know what Alfred's house is like, so huge, and chill, and standing miles away from anywhere. You can't get servants to sleep in, we tried one or two au pair girls, but they never stayed, and Alfred never came back till the small hours, and then someone offered to lend him this little house near the river. There was a woman who came in during the day and people nearby, and I told Alfred I could manage and he could come down at weekends. Anyway, we met, and I started to come alive again. It was so wonderful to be with someone who didn't think and talk and breathe money and success. I always knew it couldn't last, once he was back in college I'd start becoming unreal, well, it's the day-to-day things that create your background and everyone has to live against a background . . ."

"And Alfred was your background?"

"I suppose. Three months, I thought, I didn't expect it to last much longer—it's not a great deal to hope for . . ."

"Long enough to turn my son into a forger," I reminded her with sudden bitterness. "Whose idea was it, the check, I mean?"

She looked at me in amazement. "You can't imagine I'd have let him run that sort of risk? I'd have known Alfred would find out. When he said he'd got the money from his father—well, I did wonder why he didn't come down himself, his father, I mean—but there was this brute on the telephone threatening to show his photograph to Alfred—I couldn't let him do that, you must see." She put her hands, as small as a child's, over her face. Her rings sparkled in the gray light. "It all sounds so sordid, doesn't it? But I've wondered sometimes if Alfred wasn't behind everything."

"You mean, he paid someone to take a dirty picture?"

"It wasn't a dirty picture," she whispered.

"Compromising then."

"It's not that he needs the hundred pounds. What's a hundred pounds to Alfred? Was, I mean. I still can't think of him as dead."

"Not a hundred pounds," I told her. "Five hundred!"

She looked startled. "Oh no. Is that what he told you? It's not true. It was one hundred."

"The check, yes. But the redemption price was five."

"I don't believe it," she breathed. "Even Alfred wouldn't do that. How did you get it, though? I mean, five hundred pounds is a lot of money."

"Who says I did get it?"

"You said the police hadn't been here, but if the letters had been in his room they'd have found them."

"So they would," I agreed. "But—how did my son sign his letters?"

"Just Pip. Or sometimes P."

"And of course he didn't write from his own address."

"There was a little shop—you could have letters sent . . ."

I knew about those little shops. Their owners must grow rich on blackmail. Again I thought, My son, and winced. "Did you ever mention Philip to anyone?" I went on. "Think before you answer."

"I don't have to think." Her eyes were shining. I re-

79

minded myself harshly of will-o'-the-wisps, those danc-
ing lights that lure a man to destruction in the marshes.
"I never spoke to anyone."

I nodded. "Was it a great shock to you when you
heard your husband had been murdered?"

"I didn't believe it when they told me," she said
simply. If this was an act she was a great loss to the
stage. "I didn't think anyone would dare."

"Rich men always have enemies, and rich men who're
also blackmailers . . ."

"I didn't know anything about that. I knew about the
club, of course. Oh, he had a finger in so many pies.
You've been very kind, Mrs. Ross, I didn't think you'd
even let me in. And I promise you I won't say a word
about Philip to anyone. Only, you do have to be careful
of the police. I didn't know in England they were allowed to lay traps . . ."

"They'll tell you when you're after a wild beast no
holds are barred. You're sure no one else knows about
your affair with Philip?"

"Not unless he said anything. And he wouldn't. You
know, you mustn't think I've wrecked his life. I haven't,
no one could. That was one of the wonderful things
about him. He made you feel so safe. I'd forgotten there
was a sun on the other side of the glass, he had a sort of
faith, I don't mean religion, we never talked about
that . . ."

I knew exactly what she meant. It's a quality some
people have, but that can't, I think, be acquired. George
had had it. When our marriage broke up I knew it
wouldn't be the end of things for him. He'd much too
much vitality; he'd cross the world and put down roots
somewhere else. In a way that was my consolation now.
Come what might, Philip wouldn't let even a thing like
this break him. He was like a lighthouse, the winds batter and the birds attack, but the light goes burning on.

"He's going to need it, his faith, I mean," I said. I didn't see why I should spare her. Philip wasn't by any means out of the wood, and no matter how far his luck held, you can't change the past. He might forget about the check, but I never would. "If he gets sent down from college because of this . . ."

"I never meant to hurt him, I just wanted to give him anything he wanted. As I told you, I knew it couldn't last, but you don't draw your curtains against the sun because you know it's going to rain tomorrow."

Oh, she knew all the answers, this woman. It would have been easier for me if she'd been the calculating slut I'd anticipated. I could see no reason why Philip shouldn't go on being in love with her till Kingdom Come.

"Have they been on to him?" she asked suddenly, and I said not so far as I was aware, and I supposed I would know.

"They don't give you any warning," she said. "They suddenly appeared in the small hours to tell me about Alfred, and almost before I'd had time to accept the shock they were asking what I'd done that evening. I'd been alone, as I generally am. Alfred bought me a monster TV, but I can't put that on all the time, it's uncanny, it's like having an—an inhuman presence. Fortunately I'd called in a garage on the way. I suppose they checked up. I couldn't imagine why they should suppose I'd want Alfred dead—I mean, what good does it do me?"

"In their eyes you're now a rich widow," I pointed out.

"Instead of being a rich man's wife. I have the feeling they're still creeping and trying to discover a secret lover or something. You're sure they haven't been here?"

"I've told you. Now, Annette, I know this has all been frightful, it hasn't been a picnic for anyone, but you must agree the person to consider is Philip, and a lot's going to depend on you and me. Let him suppose you're being badgered and he'll come rushing into the open, never stopping to think he may be doing you more harm than good. Of course, if they do get on the trail there's no sense lying about it, but so far as I can see no roads lead to Oxton. No one knows I'd even met your husband —just the three of us."

She fumbled with the catch of her expensive lizard-skin bag, and pushed a card into my hand. It was so like history repeating itself, I couldn't repress a start; it was such a short time since Alfred Samson had come into my room, an utter stranger, and given me a similar card.

"Just in case anything turns up and I could help," she whispered. "There's a telephone number. You needn't be afraid of anyone else answering, the woman I had working for me walked out, she said murder wasn't nice and her husband said she wasn't to come any more."

"Are you there alone?" The question jumped up like the toad out of the mouth of the wicked princess.

"Oh, but I'm used to that," she assured me. "Alfred hardly ever got back till the small hours, and sometimes he wouldn't come back at all. That's why he had this flat in London."

"Why on earth didn't you tell him you couldn't stand it?"

"Oh well—you don't understand. The house went with the job, so to speak. I mean, he is—was—very proud of the house, but a house wouldn't be any good to him without a woman to act as mistress—a chatelaine, he used to say. He liked to bring his business friends down. Of course, I don't suppose I shall keep it now, but till things get settled, there are some advantages in being solitary. And then I liked the idea of the country, and he gave me this car." Her glance strayed to the window.

I moved across to see a very handsome pale blue car standing outside my door. I saw that and I saw something else. I saw that Miss Muir had come back from her shopping expedition and was sitting in the little communal garden the Council put up after the war in the place where two houses had been demolished by bombs. She divided her time between the window of her flat and this garden. "Always someone to talk to," she confided to me. "I always say no one in London needs to be lonely." I had a feeling she was probably waiting for an opportunity to "have a word" with Annette.

"The main thing you can do for Philip now is keep your mouth shut," I told her. "Did he ever come to Virginia Water?"

"We never met anywhere that I'd been with Alfred. No, what I really had in mind, and you mustn't take offense, you said yourself it was my fault this situation ever developed, if the police do make trouble, I mean, he might need a lawyer and they're very expensive—Alfred put a lot of his holdings in my name, it's a thing husbands do because then they can't be touched if there's any sort of crash, though no one could associate Alfred with a crash—well, anyway, you'd know where to get at me, wouldn't you?"

Fortunately at that moment my telephone rang. I snatched off the receiver. I saw Annette stiffen. She thought it might be Philip. I supposed she couldn't know much about the life of an undergraduate if she supposed he could be ringing me up at this hour on a weekend day morning.

"Gloria?" I said into the mouthpiece. "One second. My friend's just leaving."

Annette gave me an anguished, pleading look. "You

will remember? I promise not to try and get in direct touch."

"You forget," I told her, "we belong to the Welfare State. Legal advice is free, like prescriptions and crepe bandages. And another thing I thought we'd agreed. This affair is over, Philip's back at Oxton, you're in your own house, you're a widow, you can't be seen around with a boy of Philip's age. I appreciate your coming here," I added, "though I think it was mainly to ease your own mind, but now the only thing to be done is for you to melt away. There's still a chance, not a very strong one but a chance, that we can keep his name out of this."

"Unless the police find the letters and start putting two and two together. They're terribly good at that kind of thing."

"They won't find the letters," I assured her. "Your husband brought them round to me."

She stared. "I don't believe—I mean, Alfred never gave anything away without getting value."

"Perhaps he got value," I said. "But I can assure you you needn't worry about them." Of course, it ran clean counter to what I'd told her earlier, but it seemed the safest thing to say.

"You mean, they don't exist any more?"

"That's just what I mean—provided you really have destroyed the originals." The telephone began to chatter furiously. "I have to get on," I told Annette. "This is my job. Can you see yourself out? I have to get on . . ."

"Your friend seems to have been wearing her sitting breeches," remarked Gloria grimly as the door closed. I was watching the road from the window. Annette came down the stairs very slowly. I had a momentary feeling that she was hanging around outside, but she did appear, unlocked the blue car and drove away. Miss Muir didn't even see her go, she was too deep in conversation with a woman who looked like a fish standing on its own tail, tall and gray and wavering. She knows how to pick 'em, I thought.

"She had a problem," I told Gloria.

"Any use in our line?" said Gloria promptly. She was always looking for new angles in human relationships.

"Strictly confidential," I told her sadly.

"One of that kind! Listen, Margaret. We're doing a series on Women and Marriage. Yes, I know you'd think women would be sick of the subject, but somehow they never are. You know the sort of thing. The satisfied wife, the widow, the *femme sole*, the deserted wife . . ."

"How she faces her problems."

"That's right."

"She uses her guts," I said.

"We can't tell our readers that. No, what they want is to know how other women have managed in the same circumstances, they want encouragement . . ."

"A hell of a lot you care about encouragement," I said. "You simply want to put up your circulation."

"It's my job," said Gloria peaceably. "I've got one snip, a wife whose husband's just got a twenty-year sentence, and who means to stand by him."

"You're a ghoul," I said briefly. "I suppose you've got the wife whose husband is dying in hospital—or how about getting the wife of someone who's been murdered . . ."

"That wouldn't help," retorted Gloria primly. "We don't go in for sensationalism, we just want to be of some use. How many women are the widows of murderees? We can't cater to individuals . . ."

We went on like this for some time. I watched the street from my window. It occurred to me that Annette might be being followed, though even I didn't suspect Alfred of such ghostly activities. But there could be someone in the background waiting to put the black on her—only so far as I could see no one had made a move when she left my flat. There were the usual four men who were painting the house across the road, with the inevitable transistor—they never seemed to move much; there was a TV repair van; and someone was moving house, I saw the inevitable shabby furniture being brought out. A postman went past, no one else. Anyway, a car like hers would be difficult to miss. I came to abrupt terms with Gloria and hung up.

A day passed and then another day. The police didn't come to my flat, no mysterious voice called me up on the phone, I didn't even get any anonymous letters. Whoever killed Samson was lying low. The *Record* said the authorities were prosecuting their inquiries, and published an interview with the man who'd called himself Smith and had started all the trouble at the Glass Diamond. He said he'd intended to bring a charge against Samson, who owned the place, but it was just like the little twister to go and get himself murdered to avoid trouble. The fellow, he said, was a crook. The *Record,* which is always stretching its neck out, seemed to invite the chopper there. But already so much speculation and actual fact about the dead man had leaked, that no action was taken. The person most likely to take it was the widow, and she was lying as low as the female partridge that can melt into the ground and literally become invisible. Philip and I used to go around sometimes looking for them; you could step on one before you saw it.

I wondered how soon I dared return the envelope marked 27 to its owner, but common sense told me to wait till the dust had cleared. I didn't imagine the police were going to give up the case without a struggle. Their problem probably was that there were so many likely suspects, all those numbered envelopes and files. It seemed to me they might be going systematically through them, only surely the fact that the envelopes were still intact on the premises would be a proof of innocence. They hadn't found the murder weapon, and if they had unearthed any other clues they weren't telling us. If anyone had seen me going into the house, he or she was preserving a discreet silence. Not that I blamed them, no one wants to be involved with murder, and even his own guardian angel couldn't have found much good to say about Alfred Samson. Philip didn't write, but there was nothing strange about that. Annette didn't ring up either. I began to believe we might be going to go unchallenged. It seemed too good to be true.

And, of course, it was.

VI

I was going to Hanington's to buy a pair of gloves. Nowadays places like that are called boutiques and have a lot of messy little counters selling rubbish of various kinds, but old Hanington had started life as a provincial draper, and the name had meant a lot to him. When he came to London he took a little shop in an alley not far from Knightsbridge, and it hadn't changed much. I'd hardly have been surprised to find it still had a bow window. Inside it was small and rather inconvenient but you can buy the best gloves in London there, and it's the only place I know that will make buttons for the individual dress that looks as though they had been born on it. It's not cheap, but you can't have everything. Americans always took photographs of it; they called it cute. Old Miss Hanington still presided, though you didn't see much of her these days. She was old Hanington's unmarried daughter, and the London she remembered was a tourist's dream. I was always surprised to find how near Harrods we were, and the big red buses seemed to have come from a modern film and be there by mistake. There was a shop next door with purple and yellow jars of colored water in the window and a plate saying *Chymist* over the door, and there was a bespoke cobbler and an ancient jeweler. There used to be a teashop reminiscent of Miss Babington's famous teashop at the foot of the Spanish Steps in Rome, but that had recently caved in, smothered by the local trattoria and snack bars, and now it was a pet shop. But it only kept the most expensive dogs and catered for the best people. A girl with a flaxen beehive hair-do reverently took my order and old Miss Hanington tottered in and started talking about our present desperate situation, as if she referred to the Napoleonic invasion rather than our normal contemporary economic crisis. I actually forgot all about Samson, and Annette seemed no more real than a girl in a French revue. I got my gloves and ordered a belt for an astronomical price, and walked straight back into reality.

As I stepped into the street someone came out of the pet shop, with a silver poodle on a lead. A voice I'd recognize even in the grave said, "I must tell my friend. Just as a joke, of course. She thinks the world of Trixie. So that's the latest, is it?"

She stopped to stare in the window and automatically I stared too. There was only one dog on show, and that looked like a fur flea with a minute scarlet bow set in the tangles above its eyes. I've never liked very small dogs, and I couldn't imagine why anyone should spend about thirty pounds on this one. The gray poodle sniffed at my ankles and her chaperone reproved her—Trixie, that's not Nice—and, wouldn't you know, it was old Angela Muir. When she saw me she positively beamed, though I was convinced she had watched me go into Haningtons and had been spinning out her conversation until I emerged.

"I've been taking Trixie for her monthly hair-do," she confided. "Mrs. Warren is telling me poodles are Out."

She had a curious habit of accenting certain words as if they ought to be spelled with a capital letter.

"And Yorkies are in?" I suggested intelligently, looking at the minute window-specimen with dislike.

"That's it. You do get around, don't you? I mean, one can't tell you anything you don't know already. Yes, the idea is you wear out your present poodle, like wearing out your present fur coat, but you don't dream of replacing it in due course. You have a Yorkie. I was going to walk Trixie back through the park," she went on. "Why don't you come with us? You look as if you could do with a little Fresh Air."

I had made the transition from the Napoleonic era to the present day so rapidly I still felt dizzy, but I pulled myself together and said that would be Lovely, only I had a rush job on hand. I found I was beginning to talk in capitals too.

"Trixie's poor Mum," chattered Miss Muir, effervescent as Niobe as we walked towards the bus stop —I didn't dare suggest a taxi, in case she changed her mind and decided to come too. "Slipped on her own bedroom floor and broke a femur. Four days and two X-rays before the doctors realized What Had Happened. I lend a hand with Trixie, poor girl. You know," she ran on, "London must have been a lovely place when there really was a Green here. There was even a pond with geese, or so I've heard. It's all in that new book on London that's just come out. They got it for me at the public library. And Mr. Hanington's mentioned in it. He used to stand in front of his shop in a black frock coat welcoming his carriage customers. While his three daughters—he never allowed any of them to marry— served the customers."

"What about the ones who came on foot?" I asked, as we circled the little Latvian church with its barrel-shaped tower and came in sight of the park.

Miss Muir looked shocked. "Oh, I don't think there were any of those. I see they've got a man in connection with the Samson murder," she went on casually.

I was so startled, I let my bus ride away under my eyes. "Samson!" I repeated.

"Wake up, sleepy-head." Miss Muir nudged me in the ribs with an elbow not much tougher than a marlinspike. "The night-club keeper. You must remember. I can't help feeling sorry for him—this man, I mean, not Samson."

The lights changed, and we dodged across the road. I'd forgotten all about getting a bus home. "Did you realize he made his money by Blackmail?" Miss Muir hissed, like a dedicated goose. "Really, it isn't surprising someone took a poke at him."

"Rather more than a poke, surely," I murmured feebly. "Do they give him a name—this man, I mean?"

"Well, I didn't actually hear the announcement myself. Mrs. Warren heard it on that radio program where they give you the news every thirty minutes. A man has been at whatever-it-is police station assisting the authorities . . . well, we all know what that means. Assisting himself into a cell." We entered the park and she released Trixie from her lead. The poodle immediately flung herself on a wolfhound that could have devoured her in a couple of mouthfuls. "She'll be All Right," declared Miss Muir. "These dogs that get themselves born in the Atom Age must learn self-defense. It's going to be bad enough looking after the humans when they drop that bomb—no, I don't know the name but, you see, the *Record* will ferret it out. Don't ask me how they do it, second-sight perhaps. If there hadn't been a suspect they'd have invented one, and before you knew where you were the police would have accepted him as the murderer. I always thought I'd like to work on a newspaper, but of course when I was a gel parents thought they had Territorial Rights. Really, not much better than Hitler, though they'd have been shocked if you'd told them."

We walked down to the Serpentine and Trixie chased some ducks.

"You mustn't think I'm trying to be nosey," Miss Muir clattered on, "but human nature's my Hobby, and when it lives in the same house—I can't help noticing you're not quite the girl you were. That typewriter, you know," she added encouragingly, "it hasn't been clacking along as fast as usual. Oh, you mustn't think I mind the noise, I enjoy it, it's companionable. It's when it's silent—and I know you're up there—I begin to get worried. I think to myself, I wonder if she'd like me to pop up. You know, you only have to knock on the floor with a stick or something, and I'd be up quick as a wink. I've very good hearing and I'm used to keeping all sorts of hours. General Family Dogsbody, that's me." She laughed good-naturedly. "Well, every family needs one, and in the Muir family the name's Angela."

I made an excuse to part from her before we got back; she had to deliver Trixie to her owner, and I bought a paper from the old man on the corner and went home in a taxi. The paragraph, when I found it, didn't tell me much. It was the racing edition, which isn't supposed to carry any news. I bought another later in the day. The man had been allowed to go home, but you could be sure the police were keeping their beady eyes on him. His name was Spurr. At that stage it didn't mean a thing to me.

Philip telephoned that night. His voice sounded cool, but with the sort of deliberate coolness that masks agitation.

"Just thought I'd find out how you were," he said.

"Any reason I should be on the sick list?" I asked.

"Have you seen tonight's paper?"

"I've seen it," I said.

"Mum." And now the agitation was seeping through. "Have they been to see you?"

"They have not. And I'm not expecting them to. But —I suppose you'd better know this—I've had a visit from your girl friend."

I could hear his quick young breath over the phone. "I told her, in any emergency, if she needed help . . ."

"If she had the sense she was born with, or you either, come to that, she'd have kept away," I told him grimly. "The murdered man's widow can't be too circumspect, you can be sure whoever else the police may have dismissed from the case, they'll still have her in their eye."

"But she wasn't there that night."

I felt myself stiffen. "Did she tell you so?" He said nothing. "You telephoned her? Philip, you didn't go and see her that Monday afternoon before you went back to Oxton?"

"It's all right, Mum. I rang from a call box. I had to know how she was."

"I've told her to go home and keep her mouth shut. She won't try and get in touch with you, not if she's a woman of her word. There's still a chance we may be able to keep your name out of this, which means she won't be spattered with mud either. It wouldn't do her any good, you know, if it got around that she'd been having an affair with someone six years her junior . . ." I stopped abruptly; I was convinced I'd heard something, a faint breathy sound that wasn't Philip. I've been trying for years to get a separate line, it's ridiculous in my position to have to share one. It hadn't occurred to me that the old woman downstairs would deliberately listen in; now I was less sure. "Well," I said rapidly, "think it over. There's the plot to date. The trouble is I don't know how to solve the problem. I ought to have read more detective stories, I suppose, before embarking on one. If you come up with any wonderful solution . . ." After I'd hung up I wondered if I'd deceived her; for all her bunny appearance she was pretty shrewd. A lot depended, of course, on how much of the conversation she had overheard. It also occurred to me that she might have had an illuminating word with Annette when she let her into the house, only would she have been able to keep that to herself, wouldn't she have dropped a hint? I remembered some of the pictures of partisans in the war—they'd looked just the cosy old mums and aunties you tend to forget about, and they'd been about as safe as sticks of gelignite. It was a grim thought that I might have a dangerous enemy under my roof. I hadn't at that stage realized how dangerous she could be.

Of course the *Record* came up with a splendid story about the man, Mark Spurr. In all the films and books I've seen or read, the suspect buttons his lip, and if accused, reserves his defense, but Spurr was like me, he hadn't read enough. Anyway, he made a marvelous Roman hoilday for the press. It was abundantly clear that he was one of Samson's victims, which I suppose anyone would have suspected from his being pulled in at all; what became obvious to me as I read that packed column was that he was number 27. I don't know precisely how the press winkled the information out of him, but apparently he admitted he had been expecting to see Samson that night but something had intervened and he'd had to telephone to postpone the appointment. The police, by consulting a card index found in the dead man's room, could isolate individuals—they paid at regular intervals and the cards showed when those intervals were—so they'd asked for his assistance.

"I wasn't able to help them," he told the press. "I didn't go round to Maygate Street that night, and I never met anyone but Samson there when I did."

That was the gist of his statement, and I reflected he must be a near-moron to let it get that far. It was surprising in a way that I hadn't been visited, but perhaps if there was to be a sole payment, and it must have been obvious to Samson I wouldn't join his list of permanent supporters, the victim didn't merit a card. I hoped so, anyway. The report put me in a spot. Here was I, the one person who could confirm Spurr's story, and back it with proof, come to that, and I couldn't afford to speak, not unless I was prepared to sacrifice my son. I didn't think about Annette, she could have been sacrificed on the altars of Stonehenge every day for a week and I wouldn't have lost any sleep over her. All the same, it would be different if they arrested the man. I couldn't let an innocent person lie in prison under shadow of a crime I knew he hadn't committed. Or could I? I was learning a lot about myself these days, and what I learned wasn't very complimentary.

The *Record*, which never misses a trick, had a short lead on the subject of blackmail. Blackmailers, announced, were as bad as murderers, if not worse; and their victims, who refused to come forward and assist the police, were accessories after the crime, assisting a nauseating brand of wrongdoer to flourish. I thought whoever wrote that had never been in a blackmailer's power. I know about the police suppressing your name if you ask for their help, but rumors fly like bats in twilight and newspapers like the *Record* send out invisible spies with butterfly nets to catch them. The ironic thing was that I thought I was helping a fellow victim when I had removed the envelope marked 27, whereas if I'd left it where it was the police might have taken that as proof that he hadn't been in the room that night. That's the trouble with people trying to understudy God, they don't have all the facts, and it's the facts they don't know that confound them. I mulled and mulled over this problem. I had visions of Miss Muir standing in a listening attitude, with one hand cupped around her ear, waiting for the sound of the typewriter, and deciding how long to wait before she made a frontal attack. If I came to Spurr's aid, I delivered Philip to the lions. It always came back to him. Why did George have to walk out on me? I demanded of no one in particular. Other women had husbands who at least helped them to carry the can. Only I wasn't really kidding myself. I knew exactly what George's advice would be. "What are we waiting for?" he'd ask. "Get your hat and we'll go down to the station."

I decided to wait till Spurr was definitely accused. I didn't have to wait long. And now I had a fresh problem to face. Annette could only surmise that I'd been in Maygate Street that night, but Philip knew. And Philip was George's son. I heard my own silly voice saying over and over, You don't have to worry about the letters or the police or anyone. You don't have to worry about what Samson may do, because Samson's dead. I even sat for long periods trying to recall the actual words I'd used. And yet in a way you could say it was Philip who drove me to the action I eventually took. Due to me, partly at all events, he'd been deprived of one of his parents, and I don't care how much trouble you go to, the remaining one can't entirely fill the gap. Thanks to the pair of us our son hadn't got a father's protection— or at least companionship. I couldn't give him another parent who would allow an innocent man to go to jail. So at last I put on my hat and went to talk to the police.

VII

I went to the station in Cartmel Street, a stone's throw from Maygate Street, and told the station sergeant I'd like to see someone from the C.I.D. He looked as though this was happening all day, asked me my name and address and the nature of the crime I had presumably come to report.

"Murder," I said succinctly.

He took it all in his stride. "One we know about or . . ."

"One you don't know enough about. This man, Samson. I see you've arrested someone called Spurr."

"Well, that is a matter for the C.I.D." he admitted. "Were you coming to tell us you know someone else did the job?"

"How did you guess?" I asked.

"Oh, we get to hear things. For instance, there was a young man tried to get us to believe yesterday he was responsible, only it turned out he hadn't been farther south than Chester all week, and murder by remote control . . ." He shook his head. "It's all in the book, of course."

"Joke over," I said abruptly. "I happen to be able to prove it wasn't Spurr, because I . . ."

"Just a minute, Mrs. Ross." He actually waved a pencil at me as if I were a child in school. "You know you don't have to tell us anything that could prove prejudicial to your own interests."

"That's just my trouble," I assured him. "I do. You see, I was the one in Samson's room that night who took the phone call."

He thought for a moment, then said, "Perhaps you'd better have a word with the inspector." He went down a passage; I waited where I was. I don't quite know what I'd anticipated, the heavens opening or something, but certainly not this cool appraisal. I thought of the young man from Chester, and I could imagine the sergeant saying to his superior officer, "There's another nut outside, sir. Samson case. If you'd like to take a crack . . ."

The sergeant came back. "Come this way, Mrs. Ross." He took me into an office that by no stretch of imagination could be called comfortable. "This is Inspector Mall."

"Sit down, Mrs. Ross," this last offered. He was a big gangling type, very dark, the sort, I decided, who if he were on the wrong side of the law wouldn't hesitate to put the boot in.

"You've got some information for us about the Samson case?" Mall offered. The door opened and a member of the women's branch slipped in. I supposed that was more for his protection than for mine.

"I've already told the sergeant . . ."

"Now tell me," he encouraged, "but let's get this clear first. You're making this statement of your own free will?"

"No one's coercing me," I agreed.

"And you do realize that you can't be forced to say anything that might be to your own disadvantage, not at this stage, and you understand that anything you say . . ."

"May be taken down and used in evidence," I interrupted. "I've always wondered if they really said that."

"May be taken down and used in evidence," he corroborated. "Now, let's have it. We always appreciate the co-operation of the public."

"It's simply that I know Mark Spurr can't be guilty because I was in Mr. Samson's room that night when he telephoned, Spurr, I mean. He said he couldn't come because he hadn't been able to raise the money. And Samson was dead then."

"Let's get this straight, Mrs. Ross. Are you here to tell us you've someone to put in his place? Because, if so . . ."

"No," I said. "I don't know who did it, except that it can't be this man you've arrested."

"Because of the telephone call?"

Mall picked up a pencil and started to doodle, but in an idle sort of way as if he didn't know what his hands were doing. "Do you read the *Record*, Mrs. Ross?"

"What on earth's that go to do with it? Yes, as a matter of fact, I do. It's a very enterprising paper," I added.

"Gives us a lot of tips," he acknowledged. "Mind you, it's not really fair competition, we have to stick to facts."

"It is a fact," I said violently. "He did phone."

"When did you see the paper, Mrs. Ross?" He drew a mouse with a curly tail.

"I see it every day."

"But you didn't tie it up—I mean, I was wondering why you didn't come to us at once."

"You hadn't arrested him. I wasn't going to speak till then."

"I'd like to get this clear," he said. "You knew Samson was dead—you didn't lay information . . ."

"I couldn't have helped you," I protested. "I didn't know who killed him, and no one would want to advertise a call on Samson who could help it."

"I see." He drew a second mouse. "You were there on business."

"I didn't go there to ask him the time," I said tartly, and was horrified to hear my own words. "He had letters," I hurried on. "He was prepared to sell them."

"Letters you'd written?" At this stage I still hoped I could keep Philip's name out of it. Surely, I argued, it was more reasonable to believe I was the author than to suspect a boy of barely twenty. I just nodded.

"We didn't find them, did we?"

"Well, of course you didn't find them. I brought them away with me. They're destroyed now," I added. "I destroyed them the same night."

"We didn't find any money there either, except what was in the safe and a few pounds in the dead man's pocket."

"I took two hundred pounds with me, but as I told you, he was dead when I arrived. There was no sense leaving the money. I've still got it in my flat, I sold some jewelry."

"And while you were there the telephone rang?"

"Yes. I was on the point of leaving."

"And you answered it. Why?"

"I thought it might attract attention if I didn't—someone might hear, might think it odd that he didn't reply. Anyway, I wanted the bell to stop. There's something about a phone ringing . . ."

He nodded, as if he found that quite sensible. "And it was Mr. Spurr?"

"It was a man. He didn't give a name, just a number,

twenty-seven. He said he hadn't been able to raise the money, he'd bring it next week."

"And then he rang off?"

"I rang him off."

"He didn't think it odd that a woman should answer? I mean, he didn't tell us . . ."

"I didn't speak at all, I didn't have to. He broke into a spate of words. I hung up on him—well, I couldn't speak, could I?"

"There's something there doesn't altogether tie up." He drew his third mouse and went back to put a bow around the neck of the first. "The receiver was dangling when our chaps broke in."

"I thought that way, if anyone did try to ring, the bell would be silent. They might think he was there talking . . ."

"You thought of a lot, didn't you, Mrs. Ross. Kind of an alibi, did you think?"

"I didn't think I'd need one. No one knew I was going there that night. I'd never been there before."

"That explains another point, why there wasn't a card for you in the index."

"Is that how you got hold of Spurr? Went through the cards . . ."

"We have to make do with the evidence we have," he said gravely. He'd set to work drawing a cat watching the mice. "How long have you known Mr. Spurr, Mrs. Ross?"

I stared. "I don't know him at all. I'd never even heard his name till I saw it in the paper. But I'm presumably the only person who knows he didn't get in that night. Well, a dead man can't open doors, can he?"

"That's another thing. You say he was dead when you arrived. Was the front door closed?"

"You catch on fast," I said. "The point didn't occur to me till the next day. Of course someone was in the house when I got there, someone besides Samson, I mean, and I suppose it's reasonable to assume he was the murderer. Anyway, when I rang the bell someone pressed the catch." I explained about the darkened room with a door standing a little ajar.

"You told me that no one else knew you were going there that night. So why should anyone wait?"

"I suppose whoever it was—I've assumed all along it was a man—would know Samson was expecting another visitor. From what I can make out Samson made quite a profession of blackmailing."

"But this was your first visit? Did you know Samson then?"

"Not till he approached me and told me he'd acquired the letters. He'd given me till that night to get the money."

"And, of course, it was important to you to get them back?"

"It was essential. They could have done me untold harm."

"Suppose you hadn't been able to raise the money?"

"He was going to send them to a quarter where they could ruin me."

"Ruin's a strong word, Mrs. Ross. What was he asking for them?"

"Five hundred pounds."

"Five? But . . ."

"Two was the utmost I could raise. I hoped he might be prepared to accept that."

"But he wasn't?"

I remembered Annette. They come back at you and back at you. "He didn't get the chance, he was dead when I arrived."

"Who was this party he was going to send them to? Your husband?"

"My husband and I were divorced some years ago. He doesn't even live in this country any more."

"If you'd come to us . . ."

"Oh no," I said sharply. "I couldn't have done that."

"No? What was the nature of the letters, Mrs. Ross?"

I've always found that when people incessantly address you by name it exacerbates your nerves to an almost intolerable extent. "They were—of an intimate nature," I said.

"Wouldn't the person to whom they were written— you did say they were *your* letters—have helped you?"

"No," I said again. "I couldn't involve him."

"But he knew you were going to Maygate Street that night?"

"No one knew," I asserted violently.

"You mean, no one knows until now that you'd had any connection with Mr. Samson?"

I was committed to my story now, I couldn't back down. "I hadn't spoken to anyone," I said. "The whole thing came on me like a bolt from the blue. The demand, the threat—I thought they were destroyed, the letters, I mean."

He started off down another tack. "It didn't occur to you to contact us, when you found the body?"

"Of course it occurred to me. But I knew you were bound to find it sooner or later, and later didn't seem to me to matter much. I couldn't give you any positive information."

"Oh, I wouldn't say that," said Mall. "The sooner we're informed the easier it is for us—naturally. If you don't mind a personal question, Mrs. Ross—are you thinking of remarrying?"

Crazily I tried to lighten the situation. "I'm like the man who's served a term for a first offense and resolves never to get caught again."

"So that wasn't why you were so anxious to get the

letters back. You see, I can't find any reason why it should be so important to you . . ."

"I have a son," I admitted. That much was bound to come out. "If Samson had put his threat into practice—there would have been a lot of publicity—my boy's at college . . ."

"You mean, he was going to send them there? But—would he have read them?"

"Not there," I said. "But it would have been a Roman holiday for the press."

"Is that what he told you? We've muzzled the press a lot of late years. We don't allow them to report salacious divorce court details, for instance . . ."

"If you had a son of twenty," I said, "you might understand better how I felt. I had to get those papers back."

I was getting deeper and deeper into the mire. Mall continued to doodle.

"You're not holding anything back, Mrs. Ross? I mean, the police do all they can to protect the public, which means the individual, too, of course, but we can't very well do our job if we're not given the facts. There's another consideration. If you do know more than you're telling—well, concealing vital information can be a serious charge."

"If I had any idea who killed him I'd tell you," I cried passionately. "Why on earth should I want to shield the murderer—though all my sympathy might be with him? Not in this case, though."

"No?" He looked up, surprised.

"He's got me nicely in the net, hasn't he? An honest murderer would just have cleared out and made it impossible for me to enter the house."

"In which case we'd have found the letters, wouldn't we?"

I felt like a dormouse going round and round on its

wheel, a mad dormouse panting to escape and not knowing how. "I suppose you would. Would you have opened
the envelope, though? But the point doesn't arise. I went
to keep my appointment in Maygate Street, I met the
cat . . ." I stopped. "That's it. The white cat. It came in
with me."

"The *Record* made quite a point about the cat," Mall
agreed.

"To hell with the *Record*. That cat came in with me
and I can prove it."

"Now we are going places," cried Mall. "You see,
Mrs. Ross, to date you haven't given us anything we
can actually prove, not even the existence of the letters
since they're destroyed, and you won't give us the name
of the person to whom they were written. But proof."

"That cat stepped in Samson's blood, then it jumped
up on me and it left a blood imprint on my skirt. Oh,
I've had the skirt cleaned, naturally, but it was pointed
out to me by the manager of the restaurant where I
went afterwards. Tomo—that's his trade name . . ." I
supplied the address of the restaurant. "He'd remember."

"And you told him it was a cat you'd met in Maygate
Street?"

"Well, naturally I didn't. I told him it was a cat I'd
met outside the cinema."

"I don't seem to recollect your mentioning any cinema, Mrs. Ross."

"Well, I went into the Essoldo in Fairlie Street on the
way back and after that I went into Tomo's. I'm sure he
would remember."

"If you didn't leave Maygate Street till eight-fifteen
at earliest, you'd have to go to the last house, wouldn't
you? That would make you pretty late for dinner."

"The picture was nearly over when I went in. I
wanted somewhere to sit, collect my thoughts. The film

. . ." I told him the name. "I don't suppose I kept my half of the ticket . . ."

"We might think it rather queer if you had," Mall agreed gravely. He drew a Union Jack at the foot of the page. "Mrs. Ross, you're quite sure you shut the door in Maygate Street when you left?"

"Of course I did."

"So no one else could get in, unless he or she had a key?"

"Only if they broke in, like the police did."

"I ask because though there's a card made out in the name of Mr. Spurr there's no corresponding document. We work on the thesis that two and two are four, so it seemed likely someone had called for the envelope, and . . ."

"That's what I meant when I told you I had proof," I interrupted him, "only you got me so confused with all your questions. Of course you didn't find the envelope. I took it with me."

I saw I'd winded him at last. He lay back in his chair, the pencil dropping to the table in front of him. "And—did you destroy that, too?"

"How could I? It wasn't my property. It might be something Spurr wanted desperately to get back."

"And so you returned it to him?" His voice sounded like the voice of a man who's just come spluttering up from under a huge wave.

"How could I when I didn't know who he was, not till I read the newspaper report? It's at my bank in a sealed envelope. I can pick it up at any time."

I saw that under his cool air he was livid. "You didn't think to bring it with you? The only proof you had? You've let me ask all these questions . . ."

"I thought it might not be necessary to mention it," I protested. "I don't know what's inside the envelope. It could be something criminal—I don't know police procedure, I've never had anything to do with them till now," I added wildly. "I didn't want to drag him out of the frying pan into the fire. I thought they'd be safe in the bank, but if you need that envelope as proof I can get it out—one of your men can come with me to make sure it's genuine. I don't doubt he could identify it."

"How did you know it was his—a man you'd never met? If you'd consulted a lawyer before you came here . . ."

"I didn't think I'd need a lawyer. I only came to make a statement of facts . . . I found the body, I didn't realize there was anyone else on the premises—you may think that's ridiculous of me, but finding him like that was a considerable shock. I didn't stop to appreciate there must be someone else on the premises to have opened the door, I didn't even think, Did he die in a state of grace? Is he really dead? Well, I could see that, of course. What I thought was, This is the end of the line. It doesn't matter now that I could only raise two of the five hundred pounds he wanted, this is O U T. Half a dozen people could have walked down those stairs and I wouldn't have heard them. Even now I'm not here to assist the law—the law can look after itself, it's big enough surely," I continued recklessly. I felt as I used to on the Giant Dipper; you start to go down, the pace increases, the rails are steeper, people are screaming all round you, you stop being a sensible creature, you're just a victim of sensation—that's how I felt now, a victim of sensation. I couldn't stop the pace if I wanted to, I could only pray the car wouldn't crash. For an instant the whole room tilted suddenly, I put out my hand to hold the table rim. "It's so sudden," I said. "What I'm trying to say is I'm here to help him, not you."

"It does you credit," Mall congratulated me. "Seeing

you've never met him, that is. You did say you hadn't met him?"

"You know I did. Oh, I can see what you're after. Dripping wears away the constant stone." I stopped. That sounded wrong. "Isn't ordinary justice important to you?" I demanded.

Mall sighed. "Now I've heard everything," he said.

"Just for the record," I said, "what particular law am I being accused of having broken?"

"No one's brought any accusations yet, except perhaps obstructing the police in the pursuance of their duties, by not informing them when you found the body. But there'll be plenty of time for the details."

"I never thought of the legal aspect," I confessed. "I was just so glad to be out of the wood myself I wanted to help someone else. You never met Samson, did you?"

"Oh come, Mrs. Ross, you're not blaming us for that. If you or Mr. Spurr or any of those names on the index had had the sense to come to us—still, it's a fact the finer points of the law seem to escape your sex. Tell me, Mrs. Ross, what's your job?"

"I'm a free-lance journalist—and I've never written a line for the *Record*."

"I wonder how you'd like it if someone came in and just took over whatever you were doing, someone who was a complete amateur and hadn't even got her facts right, didn't know the difference, say, between a comma and a semicolon, and then asked you to be grateful."

"Oh, even I don't expect miracles," I said. "Gratitude from the police."

"You'll get that from Mr. Spurr no doubt. Does he know you've come?"

"You mean to try and trap me, don't you?" I said. "Let me refresh your memory. The only contact I've had with Mark Spurr is a brief conversation—well, it wasn't even that, as I didn't reply—the night Samson was killed."

Mall set his hands on the table top and came briskly to his feet. "The first thing to do is to recover the envelope," he said. "We'll send you along to the bank with one of our officers. While you're gone I'll have your statement typed and you can read it when you get back, and if you agree with it you can sign it."

As Crook was to observe later, you can always tell a police officer even if he's out of uniform. When we reached the bank both the pigeonholes for Investments and Enquiries were occupied, and we had to stand quite a while during which an idiot woman had the difference between pounds and dollars explained to her. At least, that's what it sounded like. There was no difficulty about my collecting the envelope, of course. I just signed for it and they ruled the entry out of the book in red ink. There were about fourteen people queueing in the bank when we arrived and about fourteen more came in on one pretext or another while we were there; and when we came out there was the usual group of stragglers on the pavement, all hoping, I daresay, to hear shots. I was surprised, though I suppose I shouldn't have been, to find that Mark Spurr was with the inspector on my return. He'd been lodged at the new Normanton jail in North London and had been brought over at Mall's request. He proved to be a tall, fair man, rather quiet in manner, not unlike George, I realized with a start, about the same age, too. When he saw the envelope his eyes nearly bulged out of his head.

"Where on earth did you find that?" he blurted.

"You can't guess?" asked Mall.

"Unless the police have been sitting on it all this while."

"This lady's been looking after it for you. Now, Mr. Spurr, can you identify it as the envelope missing from

Samson's safe—when Mrs. Ross has handed it over, that is."

"If it's not mine it's its twin brother," said Spurr grimly. "Samson used to have it on that desk of his—it was the widest thing you ever saw, you'd need to be a gorilla to reach across that. I was buying back the contents by degrees, hire-purchase, you might say. It's no wonder they call it the Never-Never."

"Then if you'll open the envelope, Mr. Spurr, and assure us that the contents are complete . . ."

Suspicion darkened his face, it was like watching the shadow of a bird of prey pass over a field of corn.

"I thought I had made it clear," he said. "The contents are of a private and personal nature."

"We want your assurance that the envelope hasn't been tampered with," Mall told him. I got the impression that for all the effect of relaxation he gave, doodling his ridiculous mice, he was nearing the end of his patience. "No one else can give us that assurance."

"I assure you I don't tamper with other people's papers," I said.

"That should be perfectly simple to prove, and then we can all relax." Mall's words were cool enough, and I must say he looked about as friendly as an icebound boa constrictor.

"The inspector," I said to Spurr, "cherishes a theory that you and I are in cahoots to defeat the law, and that I've filled an old envelope with scraps of newspaper and stuck twenty-seven on the outside . . ."

"But that's absurd," Spurr cried. "I've never set eyes on you till today."

"Ah, but can you prove it?" I was beginning to get light-headed again.

"There's one point you can easily prove," Mall told us. "And that is if the envelope in your hand is the one Samson kept in his safe. Surely it's simple enough to slit the flap. Unless you'd prefer one of us to do it for you."

The envelope was sealed with wax, and Spurr broke it reluctantly. He shook the contents onto the table surface; they consisted of three pieces of newspaper folded in two. There was no need to ask if this was what he expected to see. His eyes looked as though they were going to bulge out of his head. Then he put out a hand and picked up one of the bits of paper. It must have been sliced out of a sheet at random, it didn't even contain a complete report, a photograph, anything. He looked up, his face pale and contorted.

"I take it the answer is no," Mall said. He was the only one of us who looked perfectly at ease. This might have been the development he was looking for.

Spurr turned to me and spoke. His voice was quite different now, hard, implacable. "Joke over, Mrs. Ross," he said. "And not a very good one from the start. Where did you put them?"

I remembered the childish phrase—couldn't believe my ears. That was true of me now. "Don't be ridiculous," I cried when I could find my voice. "This is nothing to do with me. That envelope is the one I took from Samson's room, it's been in the care of the bank ever since, you can check that . . ."

"You couldn't have put it in the bank that night," Spurr pointed out. His voice made Mall sound like an ally.

"That's true. I deposited it next day."

Spurr opened his mouth, said nothing, shut it again. Then he turned to Mall. "I'm right in thinking you didn't find any documents that could have related to me among Samson's papers?" he said.

"Nothing identifiable," Mall agreed.

"So it's a case of out of the frying pan into the fire," he observed. "The only advantage about my previous situation was that at least I knew the name of my enemy. Now . . ."

"Now if you get a fresh demand you know where to bring it," retorted the inspector crisply. "You might have saved us all a lot of trouble if you'd done that in the first place." He turned unexpectedly to me. "How about it, Mrs. Ross? You're not holding out on us, I suppose?"

Between Spurr and me, the place must have seemed like a snake pit. I found myself wondering, not for the first time what that envelope should have contained. To look at him you'd have said Spurr was one of the slow-moving law-abiding crowd, not particularly bright, perhaps, but certainly not a criminal type. I wondered if anyone would say the same of me. It only proves how unsafe it is to judge a book by its cover.

"Am I really expected to answer that?" I said between my teeth. I could almost hear myself hiss.

"I don't think there's anything more to be done at the moment," Mall said, nodding to Spurr's escort. "We'll keep this envelope, since it's been shown not to be your property, and it might even prove of use to us."

"What happens to him now?" I demanded when Spurr had disappeared.

"It's more to the point, I should have thought, Mrs. Ross, what's going to happen to you?"

"Why should anything happen to me? I came here of my own free will . . ."

"With a very odd story you haven't so far been able to substantiate. I should warn you it's not healthy to try and make mugs of the police."

"Oh, surely you're not still suggesting I invented the whole story to help a man whose name I didn't know till it appeared in the press! You only had to see his face when I came in to realize he'd never set eyes on me before. As for his reaction to the envelope, that was genuine enough . . ."

"He looked astonished—yes," Mall agreed meditatively.

"That must be the understatement of the year," I congratulated him. "And I assure you I found it in Samson's room. You can ask Tomo—about the mark on my skirt . . ." I felt in another minute I'd open my mouth wide like a nightjar—you know the sort of square mouths they have, they're reputed to milk cows after dark—and yell as Philip used to do when he was a baby.

Mall turned slightly in his chair. "Barton, get Mrs. Ross a cup of tea," he said. "I daresay you could do with it, Mrs. Ross."

I giggled helplessly, surprising myself as much as anyone. "I'm sorry," I apologized, "but you sounded so like a Victorian husband—only in those days it would have been a glass of port."

"The Welfare State doesn't run to anything stronger than tea," said Mall seriously. "Mrs. Ross, this is off the record, I'd like to give you a piece of advice."

"Can I stop you?" I said. I hoped I sounded flippant, but my heart was going like a drum.

"It's extremely probable you'll be subpoenaed as a witness in due course. Before then, take my tip, and get yourself a good lawyer."

Whatever I'd anticipated, it hadn't been this. The policeman came in with two cups of tea and put one in front of me.

"You're not suggesting I'm your next suspect?" I murmured delicately.

I didn't shake Mall in the least. "I take it, Mrs. Ross, you've never been in front of an examining magistrate, let alone a judge."

"Even a judge—or a prosecuting counsel—can't eat me," I protested.

"Even in the Dark Ages men put on armor before they went into battle." Mall was still as solemn as

Athena's owl. "It didn't always save them, but it did give them a fighting chance."

"You may not believe my story," I began, but he interrupted me, as unruffled as before.

"It isn't up to me, Mrs. Ross. I'm just a cog in the machine, I have to revolve with all the rest or bring the whole machinery to a standstill. You only need a bit of fluff in the work . . . We'll send you back in one of our cars," Mall went on. "You came here as a good citizen to help us. No reason you should be out of pocket."

"It won't be necessary," I told him. I thought I'd had enough for one day without bringing the whole square to their windows by being brought back in a police car. "So long as I retain freedom of movement I may as well make use of it."

"It's for you to say," Mall agreed. "Don't forget what I said about a lawyer."

I walked out, my head swimming. When I got back to the house it was a surprise to find no rosy face pressed against the glass of the ground-floor window, one thing, anyway, I thought, for which to thank providence. But I spoke too soon. I hadn't been in more than a few minutes when something like an outsize rat came scratching at my outer door. There was no sense pretending to be out, she'd probably seen me from her seat in the gardens; she used to sit there for hours, talking to all and sundry. If anyone plotted a great train robbery in our neighborhood she'd be the one for the police to apply to, she'd have a score of clues at her fingertips. I flung open the door and there she was, white-haired, with a complexion Father Christmas might have envied, ebullient as a fine Bank Holiday morning. The instant she set eyes on me, she wagged her finger, struck an attitude and started to chant.

> *"Margaret, I'm surprised at you,*
> *You've been out with the gentleman in blue.*

> *Don't say No, you naughty storyteller,*
> *You've brought a policeman's truncheon home instead*
>   *of your umbrella.*

That was a great pantomime hit when I was a girl," she wound up breathlessly. "Saw you in the bank," she explained. "You can always tell a policeman, can't you, even in plain clothes?"

"You should have come over and joined us," I said.

"We-ell." She tipped her head to one side. "My father used to say one of the most useful faculties to acquire was a realization of when your room was preferable to your company. Seriously, my dear"—she was trying desperately hard to inveigle herself into the flat—"I hope you're not in serious trouble."

"I thought that was what we were born to as the sparks fly upwards," I countered.

"Because if you are," she went on, and I saw she'd dropped all her waggish mannerisms and was dead serious, "don't be tricked into telling them anything until you've talked it over with your lawyer."

"What a coincidence!" I said. "I've just been given that advice by someone else."

"You can't afford to disregard it." She was trying to peep over my shoulder at my sitting room, but I stood squarely in the door like the Roman soldier on duty. "I come of a legal line myself. My father used to say, Don't even acknowledge you're female, white and over twenty-one until you've taken legal advice. Facts may look perfectly straightforward to you, but it's astounding what they can be made to look like in the hands of a professional pattern-maker, which, of course, is what the police are. And lawyers, too."

"That's a very good suggestion," I said. "I shall probably act on it."

And firmly I closed the door.

VIII

My lawyers are a very impressive firm called Winter Sherborne and Winter, with magnificent offices near Bishopsgate. They're altogether too grand really to be bothered with my insignificant affairs, but you could say I inherited them from George. They were the source of the family's fortune, and I always gathered that if he could have stayed the course, there would have been room for him there, and he might eventually have become a pillar of the house. I remember George hooting at the idea.

"I've only got one life, my darling," he pointed out. "I don't want to spend it patching up other chaps' sordid quarrels."

"There is such a thing as maintaining justice," I said. "Some people even seem to think it's a noble vocation."

The seabirds on the Thames must have been startled by the roar of laughter that followed that pearl.

"Oh, Margaret," said my husband in a sort of breathy whisper, which was all he could manage, and he couldn't even manage that at once. "Justice! Remind me to buy you a dictionary for your birthday."

116

When George and I split up, this firm handled our divorce, Mr. Winter giving me to understand that this was a great favor on his part. The firm had no truck with unsavory business, but as George didn't defend and I wasn't asking for alimony, and the cause was desertion, which meant no anonymous woman in a Brighton bedroom, and as there were no bastards and no beatings-up involved, they stretched a pretty expensive point on my behalf. Similarly, when I had to buy the lease of my flat they put the bargain through. You could have acquired an estate in the time this little job has taken, Mr. Winter told me. Only if it was for free, I pointed out, in which case it should have gone through like a dream. So I couldn't be sure of my reception if I asked their advice now. But I didn't know any other lawyer, and a name like that would, I thought, impress the authorities, I even thought Mr. Winter might regard me with a certain respectful awe. After all, murder's still the capital crime, you don't get it served up to you on a plate every Sunday morning; and again, even lawyers aren't averse to publicity.

I must have sounded pretty desperate when I telephoned for an appointment because after only telling me four times it would be impossible to see Mr. Winter that day or the next, his secretary said that if I would like to come around after lunch, although he had a very tight schedule, she'd see if he could conceivably squeeze me in for ten minutes. I took a taxi from the tube station in case Mr. Winter happened to be looking out of the window, taking a breather between his crowds of clients, and it's always more impressive than toiling through the crowded pavements on foot and probably arriving with mud on your stocking and your hat over one eye. Not that I secretly believed all that blah about endless clients. George had a story of how, when he was nobbut the office boy, as he put it, and being tried out, he walked into old Sherborne's office unexpectedly one afternoon and found his boss lying down with a handkerchief over his face and a half-full bottle of port at his elbow. As George could sleep anywhere at any time and didn't like port, he decided to look about for another job, the rewards of this one didn't seem worth the sweat. Still, there was no doubt about it, the firm was doing pretty well. Walking over their fitted carpets was like wading through a field of grass. A young man called Brown met me and told me Mr. Winter would see me as soon as he could, he hoped it wouldn't be long. Mr. Winter managed to spin the time out for half an hour. I broke into my story with all the speed and grace of a cart horse plunging downhill, but I'd no sooner come to the word Murder than Mr. Winter's face went the color of a tallow candle.

"It's all right," I assured him, restraining an impulse to lean forward and pat his hand. "I haven't murdered anyone, I don't think I'm even a suspect. But I may have to give evidence at the inquiry and/or the trial—the Samson case," I added, since he seemed all at sea.

Young Mr. Brown, waiting like an Edwardian footman behind his employer's chair, interposed rapidly, "The night-club proprietor, knocked on the head in Bayswater. A man's been detained."

"Who didn't do it, but I'm the only person who can prove that, except of course the actual murderer, and you'd hardly expect him to come forward, and before I have to face the barrage I thought it might be an advantage if I had the backing of a firm of your reputation . . ." I heard a shocked breath behind me—Mr. Brown again—but I paid no heed. Downhill I went, hardworking old cart horse, clip-clopping fit to beat the band. Out came the details—the same edited version I'd given the police, of course. I still stuck to the notion that I could make everyone believe I'd written the letters, that

Philip knew nothing, I didn't see how he could come forward and make me appear a perjuror, if it ever got that far. And he'd naturally be pleased to keep Annette's name out of the case. "I'm new to this sort of thing," I wound up, regardless of Mr. Winter's stricken face. "It hadn't occurred to me before that it could be just as dangerous being innocent as being guilty, if you lacked the necessary proof."

When I ran down for loss of breath Mr. Winter spoke. "I am not altogether clear what you are trying to tell me, Mrs. Ross. In any case, this firm does not handle criminal cases. If you have information in regard to Samson's death that you consider the police should know . . ."

"They do know," I howled. It sounded like a banshee whistle. "That's what I'm trying to tell you. It was they who advised me to come to you."

For a moment there was a complete silence. Mr. Brown poured out a glass of water and brought it to me. I wondered what I was meant to do with it—pour it over the goggling Mr. Winter?

"You say you have been to the police?"

"Yes—yes—yes." I began all over again, the appointment, the phone call, the envelope lodged at the bank—I must have been coherent this time, because he seemed to find some sense in what I was saying. But there was no question of his liking what he found. You could almost see him, like Pontius Pilate, washing his hands. Before I got to the office I'd been forced to realize I was in something of a spot. Mr. Winter made me understand that that spot might be the size of a jungle in which I could be impenetrably lost.

"A skeleton," I said suddenly. "A skeleton in the wilderness."

Mr. Winter jumped again. Mr. Brown offered him the discarded glass of water, and said, "Do I understand you to say that you yourself are under suspicion?"

"How can I be under suspicion when he was dead when I got there?" I demanded. "Only if I had some reliable backing, the sort a firm like this could provide . . ." I wanted to add, Then I could be dead sure of falling off the cliff edge, but even my limited discretion silenced me there.

Mr. Winter was getting his second wind. "As I explained to you earlier, Mrs. Ross, this is not the type of case my firm could conceivably handle. I could suggest your consulting Messrs. King and Thorbury, a very reliable connection—if it should turn out that you require counsel, a fact I think we have to face, then no doubt Sir William Overbury or someone of equal standing—" He let that sentence hang in the ear. "As I have said, you would get better advice from them."

"I suppose Sir William Overbury comes at about a thousand pounds a yard," I said brutally. "My assets at the moment are two hundred pounds raised with the greatest possible difficulty." I thought it was too bad the times were gone when sensational press lords offered to stand your expenses and give you something on the side for your trouble. "Moreover," I went on, "I've not been accused of anything yet. It doesn't say much for British justice if I'm expected to run into a debt that'll be round my neck till I go down into the pit, in order to show I didn't commit a crime I never thought of committing and didn't, in fact, have the opportunity to commit, since someone else got there first."

"I think," said Mr. Winter faintly, "you had better consult Mr. King. I will have a word—he can outline the situation to you better than I—naturally Counsel's fees would be consonant with his abilities, in Sir William's case quite exceptional . . ."

"I suppose they'd give me legal aid," I said. "A *femme sole* with a son still at college." All the same, I saw my hopes of keeping Philip out of this receding. In my mind's eye I saw his name on every billboard: READ THIS WEEK'S SUNDAY *Liar*. ACCUSED WOMAN'S SON SPEAKS. I was surprised to find I'd traveled far enough in about a quarter of an hour to contemplate myself in the dock. Mind you, you couldn't blame the Sunday *Liar*. Annette's picture alone should be good for ten thousand readers.

Someone rang on the intercom. "Mr. Winter, your next appointment . . ."

"You will be hearing from me," Mr. Winter promised hastily. Mr. Brown, who was wasted in these surroundings and would have done a treat in the Diplomatic Service, got me across the room and out of a side door before about six thousand pounds' worth of mink plunged into the room.

"Well, that was nasty, brutish and short," I commented as we waited for the lift. "Tell me, Mr. Brown." I looked at him thoughtfully. He was older than Philip, of course, but not by too many years. "What would you do in my shoes?"

He sent a sharp darting glance this way and that and over his shoulder. I didn't blame him for his caution, it wouldn't surprise me to know every panel of this elegant passage was bugged.

"Don't quote me, Mrs. Ross," he said, "and I'd get my cards overnight if Mr. Winter knew, but—just my opinion, of course—I'd say King's was as much good to you as a sour apple. For this kind of thing, which is a bit tricky, you don't really want a plushy lawyer, someone with a reputation to maintain, I mean . . ."

"I know exactly what you mean," I said. "What I want is a man who'll be concerned about my reputation. Who's your bet?"

"Well." His voice dropped lower than ever. "I say, this lift seems to have stuck—should we walk down?" He didn't wait for my reply. "There's a man called

Crook," he said. "This sort of case is meat and drink to him."

"As well as bread and butter?"

"He's not the kind of chap that has much truck with bread and butter, but when he wants it he always knows where to look for it. If he thought your fridge was understocked he'd get it out of someone else's, and stay on the right side of the law."

"Why didn't Mr. Winter recommend him then?"

"Did you ever hear of the local bishop recommending a traveling tinker? I don't suppose John Bunyan got much support." He stopped abruptly. "I talk too much."

"Not for me," I told him. "What you're trying to tell me is that Mr. Crook can bend the evidence to suit the individual curve."

Mr. Brown chuckled. "He'd rather enjoy that way of putting it."

"I hope you're right, that he bends his financial demands in the same ratio."

"You won't have to worry about money," Mr. Brown assured me. "He'll take what he can get, of course, but if your funds run out halfway, he won't be the one to suffer, and the client who pays the other half of the bill will never guess."

"He must have a very good accountant," I murmured.

"Oh, Crook has the best of everything. He even drives a Rolls-Royce." He chuckled again. At that stage I didn't understand why. From the stairs above someone called Mr. Brown's name. "Here's the address," said young Brown. "One twenty-three Bloomsbury Street, no appointment needed, no introduction either, come to that. And no need to ask him to keep the conversation under his hat, because it would never go through his mind to tell the police anything. It's like those two Scottish clans, the Macdonalds and another, who never spoke except with the dirk." He jumped into the lift, whose door had been left open, and soared out of sight.

I walked out into the street, where mysteriously the sun seemed to have come out. I took a tube train to Southampton Road and started to walk down Bloomsbury Street. Number 123 was the shabby end. The house, which was tall, narrow and had no lift, had a Dickensian sootiness that somehow was reassuring. I've been here a hell of a long time and I'll be here when you're dead and buried, the house seemed to say. Mr. Crook's office was on the top floor. I thought only a very successful man could expect his clients to climb five flights of badly carpeted stairs. At the top I was met by a tall thin man with a look of elegant cynicism gone to seed. He didn't look as if he could spell the word Law, but at a glance I realized he could run rings around Mr. Winter. But it turned out that he wasn't the lawyer I'd come to see, but his partner, a man called Parsons. He opened an inner door and signed to me to walk in. He hadn't even asked my name. I thought perhaps Mr. Brown had telephoned. I even began to wonder if this was the right place, after all. Behind the most cluttered desk in London sat a solid square figure who looked as if he might have been lifted out of an exhibition of modern statuary. Big head covered with gingery hair, big red face, every feature slapped firmly on and defying the atom bomb to change their shape or location, huge shoulders under a bright brown coat—part of a suit, I realized, when he stood up—immense hands—ex-pugilist, you might have thought, only gone a bit heavy for the job, something to do with turf accountants, perhaps, as innocent of scruple as a newborn mouse of hair. He got to his feet as I came in. Even his shoes were bright brown. It was like seeing the Rock of Gibraltar shake itself and start to rise.

"Come right in, sugar," he said. He offered me the sort of chair that even in these days gets given away for five bob at street auctions. "Personal recommendation, or you just saw the name on the door?" (So young Brown hadn't rung up, after all.)

"Personal recommendation," I said. And stopped.

"No names, no pack-drill." Mr. Crook beamed. "Funny, you know, how often you never hear the names of your best friends. In a bit of trouble?"

"The worst," I agreed.

"That's the sort I like," said Crook. "Stops you getting rusty in the joints. Well, give, sugar, what is it? Murder, G.B.H., forgery, larceny, abduction."

"Murder," I said. "And the old family firm's buttoned into its strait waistcoat of respectability so tight it won't touch it."

"Husband?" asked Mr. Crook sympathetically. "Don't mind telling me. I know it happens."

"Not in this instance. He's in New Zealand—my husband, I mean—ex-husband," I corrected.

"He who fights and runs away lives to fight another day. Lot in that, sugar. Boy friend then?"

"If you've read the papers this week you must know—it's the Samson case."

"That one?" said Crook. "They've taken a chap . . ."

"Who didn't do it. And I can prove it. But no one believes me."

"More to the point if you could prove who was guilty."

"Well," I said. "How am I supposed to do that? I don't know."

"That clears up that point." He let out a deep breath. It was like watching one of those rubber pigs slowly deflate. "For one hideous moment I thought you were going to tell me you were responsible. Police on your tail?"

"I've been to them. It was they who advised me . . ."

"To come to me? Oh no. I'm like Lewis Carroll's White Queen, I can believe six impossible things before breakfast, but never that the police sent you here."

"Well, of course they didn't. They said to get legal advice. And I got a tip—I've no more idea than the man in the moon who killed Samson, though I should think there are plenty who'd have been glad of the opportunity, but as I was the one who found him and didn't report it, I thought a little legal backing . . ."

"You thought right," agreed Crook with feeling. "They're a shocking lot, the police, no holds barred, give them a ha'porth of evidence and they'll weave you a shroud in thirty minutes flat."

"I only went to them because Spurr's an innocent man," I repeated. "How could I guess they'd think it was a plot between us, that it could have been a plot between us, I mean—he was as horrified as I was . . ." I stopped. The room had suddenly began to swim. I reflected that I'd had practically no food today and had been subjected to one nervous shock after another. Crook put a hand about the size of a leg of mutton over mine.

"I don't have one of these electronic brains," he assured me patiently. "I find it's easier to follow a story if I start at chapter one. So let's do that, and turn your watch over till you're through. We've got all the time there is. So, give, sugar, only—don't leave out the awkward bits—if there's a boy friend or anything involved—no one supposes you went to Maygate Street just for a glass of sherry—lay it all out on the table."

So carefully I repeated my story. "All this philanthropy!" Crook sighed. "And all to help a stranger. If you'd left the envelope where it was . . ."

"I thought I was doing him a favor," I protested.

Crook sighed. "They always do." He looked at me questioningly.

"That's all," I said. "I did hope you'll represent me if it should come to that."

"I don't know who sent you," Crook said, "but you've been misled. I mean, I ain't no Israelite. Oh come, sugar, you remember who the Israelites were—the chaps who were expected to make bricks without straw. Now, I can turn you out a classy brick with as little straw as any man living, but I can't do it on nothing flat. I'll give you a bit of advice for free," he added. "It's no use trying to call in a lawyer if you don't trust him. He knows it, you know it, and in about five minutes the whole court's going to know it. Well, been nice meeting you." He was on his feet again.

I was riveted where I sat. "I don't understand."

"Sapphira was slain for less than that. Mind you, I can see you're new to the game. You need a lot more experience before you'll be a convincing liar. And remember, you can commit crimes of omission as well as the other sort."

"I've told you what happened . . ."

"I never did go for these expurgated editions. You've told me you were bein' blackmailed on account of some letters you'd written to person or persons unknown. I take it you weren't selling your country down the river?"

"Well, of course not."

"And you weren't plannin' a second bank robbery?"

I shook my head.

"So what had Samson got on you? You're free, white and twenty-one. You weren't betrayin' a husband—I take it the letters were of an amorous nature? Yes, I thought so—because you'd already put him among the discards—so why shouldn't you be writing love letters to the Archbishop of Canterbury if you were so disposed." His huge face suddenly lighted up. "I take it it wasn't to him?"

"Well, of course it wasn't." I hesitated. "There was a check as well. I hoped that needn't come out."

"Signed by?"

"Ostensibly signed by Samson."

"And actually signed by you? No, sugar, I don't buy that one either. Why, you told me yourself you'd never so much as heard his name till he came to your flat. If they were love letters," he went on thoughtfully, "they weren't written to a dame, which puts Mrs. S. out. I suppose the truth is they were written by your idiot son, who seems to take after his mother. Well." He slammed his great fist on the table. "Why couldn't you say so to start with?"

"I didn't want to implicate him," I burst out.

"Seeing he's implicated himself—don't tell me he was having himself a ball with Samson's wife?"

"Samson's own words."

"Why couldn't you say so to start with? Now let's have the unexpurgated edition. And remember, from now on, I charge by time."

Really, it's surprising that so many people tell lies when the truth is so much simpler. My new version of the story, which stuck to the facts, took about half the time to tell. Crook stopped me once or twice—he wanted to know what I'd done with the check. He didn't doodle as Inspector Mall had done, just sat there looking like a great mahogany Buddha.

"That's more like it," he approved when I'd finished. "Mind you, there's still some gaps, but that's what you're paying me for, to fill them. Which version did you give the police?"

"The original one."

"Always a pity to get in Dutch with them when we may need their help later. Who did you see? Mall? He's no fool, he'll have rumbled you. What did he draw while you were talking?"

"Mice," I admitted, "and a cat."

"I'd be sorry for any mouse that got in his path. Still, you've got a cat of your own now." The telephone rang and he answered it. "Wrong number," he said cheerfully. "I'm not in the running for the Perjury Stakes just now." He hung up and grinned. "Another of those chaps who thinks if you can grease a lawyer's palm enough he can prove you were in Newcastle when fourteen witnesses and two police constables know you were in Carnaby Street the night a shop got done. You know, sugar, in every case you'll find some detail, something that don't fit the rest of the pattern, stands out like a sore thumb. When you know the reason for that you're on the road to discovery. Take this Samson affair. Know what foxes me? Why didn't he defend himself when he saw death rushin' at him armed with a tomahawk or whatever? He had this gun in the drawer— mind you, if it had been me it 'ud have been on the desk, but could be he thought he'd trap one of the larger anthropoids one of these days— Long arms, see?" he added kindly. "Reach across any desk ever made. But he don't seem to have done anything, didn't even get up from his chair—well, it wasn't shoved back like it would be if he tried to rise—just sat there waiting to be clobbered. It don't make sense to me."

"Perhaps it all happened so fast," I suggested rather feebly.

"Thought you said you had to walk a quarter of a mile from the door to the desk. A chap rushing at you to bash out your brains don't move like a snowflake. Besides, a blackmailer looks up the instant the door opens. He may look down again the next second, but he has to guard against the thousand-to-one chance that this time his man's brought a witness with him. Mind you, that don't often happen. Chaps who're being blackmailed know a secret stops being a secret when anyone else muscles in. You could say it wasn't a secret any longer when the blackmailer knows, but you get my meaning. And then if there should be trouble, like you scalp the blackmailer, say, what have you done? Laid yourself open to blackmail from another quarter."

"If it was a friend . . ."

Crook shook his head. "Maybe that kind of friend exists in a better world where there ain't no police state, but your man who's being blackmailed trusts no one. Well, look at you. Didn't even trust me enough to give me the facts when you came through that door, and I'm the one you're looking to to pull you out of the con-sommé. Besides, there's the atmosphere, the atmosphere of fear, of desperation. It's something you can smell, even animals know it. Samson knew it, too; he didn't put himself behind that barricade just for fun. He was like St. Paul, knew he stood in jeopardy every hour."

"Then perhaps it was someone he'd known a long time, someone with whom he felt so safe . . ."

"You can't have been listening, sugar. Chaps wearing Samson's shoes are never safe, and they know it. Cars run off pavements, chaps shove on the platform just as the train comes in, you get a lift in a car with a perfect stranger, so you think, till he turns his head under a street lamp . . ."

"He *couldn't* lift his head when I came in," I recalled.

"There could be a reason for that," Crook reminded me. "You are giving me the works this time, aren't you? I mean, that gun really was in the drawer . . ."

"It was in the drawer," I confirmed. "I noticed it specially because it was the spitting image of one I used to have . . ."

"Hey, hey, you must have forgotten that bit. What was a nice lady like you doing with a gun?"

"My husband gave it me—oh, years ago—when I was alone a lot in a solitary cottage. I never fired it except in practice, I used to keep my eye in . . ."

"I like a dame that don't leave anything to chance. Your husband must have been a brave man," he added simply.

"So brave he walked out on me," I agreed. "Anyway, after I parted from George, I parted from the gun, too."

"Round about the same date?"

"No," I agreed. "Not then. As a matter of fact, most of the time I forgot I had it."

"What made you remember? Now, sugar, no more aces up the sleeve, please. How did you part from it?"

"I lost it."

His big red brows climbed his forehead. "Not so easy to lose a shooter," he offered. "Tell me, this lad of yours —he know you had it?"

"I told him, but he never fired it, even in fun."

"I never saw much fun about firing a live bullet," Crook acknowledged. "Keep it loaded?"

"Of course not."

"Any ammunition knocking around?"

"Oh yes—George supplied me with some in the first place."

"Happen to mention the gun to the police?"

I shook my head.

"Licensed?" He was like a boll weevil or something that goes on boring and boring till your foundations collapse.

"It was for years, but—well, I tell you I forgot about it."

"This lad—what's his name? Philip—he forget?"

"If you're trying to tie him up with Samson's death, you can do some forgetting," I cried hotly. "He wasn't even in London, he was en route for Oxton."

It was hard to shake Crook. "Coming from?"

"He'd been down with me for the weekend."

"And—he knew about Samson?"

"He knew he'd been to see me."

"Bringing the letters. Shook him a bit, I wouldn't wonder. Now, sugar, bite on the bullet, if you think you can keep your son out of this you're dafter than most dames. How about the others in the picture? Lady-wife?"

"She's got an alibi all wool and a yard wide. Called at a garage near Virginia Water that evening."

His eyebrows went up again, they made me think of those big woolly bear caterpillars going up a fence.

"Who says?"

"She told me herself."

"That's something else you forgot to mention, meeting her, I mean."

"She came, after the murder, to find out if I'd kept my appointment with her husband."

"So she knew about that?"

"They were her letters."

"What did you tell her?"

"That he'd told me there was no sense going unless I could take the five hundred pounds. And as I hadn't been able to raise even half that sum, I left her to draw her own conclusions."

"You don't mind taking chances, do you?" murmured Crook. "Think she believed you?"

"I don't know why she shouldn't."

"But she didn't say? Shows her good sense. Where murder's in mind, the less you know about it the better. This chap, Spurr—any special reason you should remove the envelope?"

"I didn't think of it till after I'd spoken to him. He sounded so—driven—it was a fellow feeling, I knew exactly what it was like—and the envelope was there."

"Does you credit," said Crook. "Only you mustn't be

surprised if the police don't take it that way. They'll ask, as who wouldn't, why you should take a chance like that for a puffick stranger."

"I've told you."

"And I daresay you told them. Now, I could believe you because you're my client, but they'll start lookin' round for another motive, and it wouldn't be hard to find."

"Their suggestion," I told him recklessly, "is that we were in it together."

"Could be. He does the job and stops to let you in, you find the corpse, he phones to break his date, knowing you'll report it to the police—probably got an alibi of his own from eight-thirty onwards. Point is, where's the real number-twenty-seven envelope. We'll be a lot further on when we know that."

"It doesn't make sense," I objected. "No one would enter into that sort of compact. They'd know it was bound to recoil on them."

"Very unusual criminals if you did. Weakness of wrongdoers, all those who're picked up, anyway, is they only look one step ahead, and then go charging on. Never seems to go through their minds it could be a case of Here Be Dragons when they turn the corner."

"But surely *you* don't believe . . ."

"Stop asking silly questions, sugar. You're my client, ain't you, and I only work for the innocent. Now, tell me, who else knew you were coming here today?"

"Only young Mr. Brown. Well, I didn't know myself till I was leaving the office. I didn't even know . . ." I stopped abruptly.

"Cat got your tongue?" inquired Mr. Crook in polite tones. "Didn't even know there was such a chap as Arthur Crook. Well, that goes to show what a blameless life you've led to date. No one's heard of me till he's up against a wall, facing a firing squad, or he's had a pal in that position. Wonder who Brown's pal was. Oh well, they come and go, can't remember everyone. Now, I know this is a counsel of perfection, but do you think you could manage to keep your trap shut, even to your son, till I give the word? Nothing bugs me more than losing a client."

"I couldn't blame you," I agreed meekly. I meant it, too. No money, no references and prepared to lead him up the garden from the word Go.

"You're not with me, sugar. If I was to lose you it 'ud be because you weren't in a position to blame anyone. Just put on your specs and view the landscape o'er. You know this chap Spurr didn't kill Samson, because Samson was dead when he phoned. You didn't do it, because you're my client. Mrs. S. was a county away, and clever though we are nowadays you need to be something very special to be able to dot your old man over the head by remote control. It wasn't your lad, because he was either in Oxton or speeding thither—I daresay he could show that, if need be—which leaves X. The only other chap in the picture, so far as we've got it, is the one who took the photo, and even he's only a probable starter because no disinterested person ever saw it. Still, he's all we've got. Now, if you could get yourself permanently silenced, X would be sitting pretty. If your word gets Spurr off the hook it's up to the rozzers to find a replacement."

"I'm not sure they don't have their eye on me," I told him humorlessly.

"You could do worse. At least you'd be safe in quod."

"You can't imagine Philip would take that lying down? He'd come bursting into the station, flinging the truth to the four corners of the earth, wouldn't stop to think. He's like George there."

"How about Annette?"

"It's a funny thing," I said, "because he'd risk his own

life and future for her, but if I was accused he'd expect her to carry her share of the can. Don't ask me how I know that, I just do."

"A good point," Crook approved. "One more thing that may not have struck you, you don't know what X looks like, it's even an assumption that he's a male—don't forget the Amazons, who were said to be more terrifying than any male who ever lived—but he has the advantage of you. He had to be on the premises to let you in, so he'd get a gander at you while you hesitated about invadin' Samson's privacy. Mind you, he could have found out before—or it could be he just chanced his arm, had no more notion than the man in the moon who the next visitor would be, but he could just conceivably put the finger on you. Which means," said Crook, warming to his task, "he could be tagging you without you knowing. How did you get here?"

"Tube and my own feet. I took a taxi to Sherborne, Winter . . ."

Crook dismissed Sherborne, Winter with a wave of his huge hand. "That lot couldn't catch a baby butterfly in an outsize net. I know about them. Probably in the clear to date, you, I mean, or you wouldn't have reached the top floor in one piece. Now is when you have to play it cagey. Who else lives in your house?"

"The top floor's empty at the moment, people abroad; three girls have the basement, only they never seem to be in before about two A.M. and of course there's Miss Muir."

"Tell about her," Crook invited.

"There's not much to tell. She occupies the ground floor and gets her thrills, such as they are, at second hand. Sits at the window, you know the type."

Crook beamed. "Thought they were a dying race. Age group?"

"Around about sixty. Plus rather than minus. Buys

her clothes at the jumble sale, from the look of them. Ears like an elephant . . ."

"And an eye that never sleeps. And I thought they didn't exist any more."

"They do where I live," I assured him. "I bet there's many a coven of witches turn out on Walpurgis Night, she might even be one herself. She must have had more keyhole practice than an army of Peeping Toms," I wound up recklessly.

"Better and better," said Crook. "That's the kind that's the policeman's friend. You should cultivate her."

"And we share a party line," I wound up. "I don't say she listens in, but she could."

"I'd listen in myself in her place," commented Crook unscrupulously. "The things that happen to you. Don't forget her kind can be a pretty useful number, so long as they're on your side, of course. Virtually invisible, see, and the invisible witness is often the most useful kind there is. Besides, if she's keepin' an eye on you she'll notice if you don't turn up one night, and out with her broomstick and off to the police station. Well, sugar, remember, mum's the word. I'll be seeing you. Don't get a sudden inspiration and start up a rival office, will you?"

"Don't call us, we'll call you," I quoted.

"That's the idea. Remember Mahomet that wouldn't go to the mountain?"

"So the mountain came to him."

"That'll be the day," beamed Crook, "that'll be the day."

He came buzzing around the side of his cluttered desk, marked with burns and the stains of glasses, like some enormous bumblebee, to show me out. The man, Bill Parsons, was talking on the telephone; he didn't even lift his head to see me go.

IX

For the next day or so I felt like Bunyan's Apollyon when he watched the burden from his shoulders rolling downhill. I sent Mr. Sherborne a note to say not to worry about Mr. King, I was making my own arrangements. I hoped young Mr. Brown would get the message and realize how grateful I was. It occurred to me that Mr. Crook hadn't said anything about expenses, beyond his warning that he charged by time, but I didn't let that bother me either. I caught up with some work that had been outstanding ever since this miserable business began; I thought of ringing Philip but decided against it, I thought it would be too much of a temptation to mention Crook's name. When I went out I developed a rather odd habit of suddenly turning my head or stopping to fix a shoe while I took a lightning glance round me, but if I was being followed it was being done pretty skillfully. When I met Miss Muir in the hall she said earnestly, "I hope, my dear, you have thought carefully over what I said the other day about a lawyer," and I told her, "Any other police wallah who turns up you can refer to Mr. Crook." She gave quite a girlish giggle.

"He sounds like somebody's umbrella," she said. "More like a shepherd," I assured her.

And then suddenly everything blew up.

It started with a phone call. I had met Miss Muir (as usual) and she had said in her most urgent voice, "Am I glad to see you, Mrs. Ross? Your telephone's been ringing like nobody's business, as they say. It does so Worry me to hear a phone ring on and on—I always feel it may be something Urgent."

"A matter of life and death," I agreed solemnly.

"You know, I'd be only too glad to act as your unpaid private secretary, just Take your Calls, and Bring up your Letters, if you were out. I've always wanted to Write, myself." (They always do.) "Not that I haven't tried. Who was that man who said he papered the wall of his den with rejection slips?"

"A liar, I should think," I told her. "And it's very kind of you, but I always say if it's anything important they'll ring again." I could imagine her having a whale of a time snooping around my flat in my absence.

"It might be someone just Passing Through," she urged wistfully. "At least then you'd know they'd remembered you."

"There's always an automatic calling service," I reminded her, and she nodded.

"Quite uncanny, isn't it? So strange that the mores of one generation were the crime of another. Think how many witch fires would be burning in the Middle Ages if someone had produced a Computer or even a Flying Machine."

I left her to her imaginings and went up to my flat, where I sat willing the telephone to ring again. It might be Philip, I thought. Or, more probably, Mr. Crook. But when it did ring at last it was neither of them. The voice was a bit brusque, quite young, and it asked bluntly, "Can I speak to Phil?"

At least, I reflected, it was masculine, though it isn't always easy to tell these days, any more than you can always be certain about the sexes so far as appearance goes, what with all the girls in jeans and the men tying back their locks with hair ribbons.

"Who's speaking?" and the voice said, "Is that Mrs. Ross? This is Roy."

Roy Frampton was the undergraduate who shared Philip's digs. They had been promised quarters in the college next year, meantime they were lodged with a frowsy old dame who probably drank their sherry when they had any, and read their letters. When I said as much to Philip he only laughed and retorted, "Well, Ma, you have been warned. If you want to pass on secrets you must develop a code."

"Of course it's Mrs. Ross," I said. "What gives you the idea Philip would be here?"

"You mean he isn't?"

"Of course he isn't." Then the implications of what he had said dawned on me. "Do you mean he's not at Oxton?"

"He came down on Friday night." The voice sounded puzzled. "He had this message."

"Asking him to come and see me?"

"Saying he was wanted—I thought perhaps it was an accident. I mean, it was urgent—and he looked pretty upset."

"How did he get the message?" I demanded, and Roy said, "By phone. He said he had to leave right away. I loaned him three pounds, it was all I had."

"You must be spoofing," I suggested, and at once his voice took on a frosty note. He was just the opposite of my son, small, dark, intense, and as earnest as a Welsh divine's sermon. Come to that, I believe he had a Welsh divine in his ancestry.

"This is serious, Mrs. Ross. At least he thought so.

Said he must catch the next London train, he'd leave his bike at the station. And it's still there. I checked." Philip doesn't have a car, but has to make do with one of those low-slung machines that look like racers and can slide in and out of traffic as the smallest car couldn't do. A lot of Oxton men have them; you see them locked in their scores outside the railway station.

"Then it's Philip who's pulling your leg," I told him, "because I didn't send any such message. I can't imagine why he should suppose I would."

"He's been very anxious about you, since this breakdown . . ."

"Since this what?" The telephone receiver nearly jumped out of my hand and hit the ceiling.

"He feels responsible," Roy labored on.

"He could have fooled me," I said.

"You being a widow, to all intents and purposes. You mustn't mind his having confided in me," went on that serious priggish young voice, "it's better to talk to someone. And where it's a case of illness . . ."

"Illness?" I snorted. How like my idiot son. He couldn't give me a normal thing like appendicitis or pneumonia, no, it had to be a breakdown, with me teetering on the verge of a lunatic asylum, and no thanks to him I wasn't already over the threshold. "If I were having a nervous breakdown," I said more calmly, "which, in fact, I am not, ask Philip who's responsible." And then without any warning I began to laugh, because the notion of Philip as my guardian angel was really funny. Roy, however, saw no humor in the situation.

"But if he didn't come down to you, Mrs. Ross, where did he go? I mean, you can't just walk out of college for a weekend . . . And why should he tell me you were the reason?"

That brought me up with a jolt. "You may have something there," I agreed. Suddenly I was sick with anxiety. "He can't have met with an accident."

"I should think if he had they'd have notified you. They'd certainly have notified the college."

"If they knew who he was."

"But he'd be bound to have some mark of identification." Roy sounded shocked. "He took an overnight bag with him, he'd have his name on his shirts or something."

I didn't speak. I buy Philip's things at Marks and Sparks, and I'm not so careful about name tabs as I should be. And, of course, he wouldn't have a driving license. Still, he'd have a railway ticket from Oxton, which would mark him as a student there. My panic subsided a little. "Yes, of course," I agreed.

"And you'd have been notified," Roy's voice plodded on.

"I suppose he thought it would be easier to get leave if he said I'd sent for him," I murmured, thinking aloud. "He wouldn't expect you to check up. All the same . . ."

"You mustn't let it worry you," Roy said. He intended to be a doctor, I could just hear him trying to soothe his more hysterical patients. "One thing, he's not the suicidal type."

"Have you gone bonkers?" I demanded. "Why on earth should you suppose that my son . . . ?"

"I said he *wasn't* that type. Well, I'm sorry to have disturbed you, Mrs. Ross. And I wouldn't worry. He's sure to be back tonight, want my head on a charger if he thinks I've bothered you."

"Why did you ring up?" I asked.

"He promised to bring back a book of mine he borrowed a good while ago and left in your flat. I just wanted to remind him."

"Tell me the name of the book and I'll post it," I

said. "It's probably your only hope of ever seeing it again."

He told me and I wrote down the title and forgot all about it at once. As I hung up the receiver I thought I heard a faint click. I was pretty sure what that meant—someone else had been listening on the party line, and that could only be Miss Muir. I remembered her saying once that she hoped she didn't interfere with my work, sharing my telephone. Not that I use it much, she'd said, but of course, it's different for you. Sometimes when I pick up the receiver, you always sound so enthusiastic—not that I listen in, of course, when I realize the line's in use—but that's a virtue one sees so little of these days. Everyone so lackadaisical . . . I could hear her voice chattering away like an animated ghost.

If she had been listening in, she'd have a marvelous time, telling all her friends and acquaintances in the Gardens about my son running from the police—that was the least she'd make of it after my being brought back by them—or she might suggest he'd eloped. I tried to remember if Annette's name had been mentioned, but, of course, it hadn't. Probably Roy had never heard it. Whatever else the old witch was short of it wasn't imagination. Not that I needed much of that to guess where my son was, there was only one place he could be. I felt I could kill that woman, dragging him back into the mess when I'd been at such pains to pull him out. As for her promise to darling Alfred—but I suppose she'd think death released her from that. I wondered what on earth she could have told him to bring him down at such a rush. Naturally, I hadn't been expected to know anything about it, being a weekend would seem a marvelous opportunity and he'd be back, bright and shining as a cherub, on Monday morning.

I dug out the card she'd left me, with her name and address, and rang up Boxwood House, but either they'd gone out or she wasn't taking any chances answering the phone. Anyway, no one did.

Two can play at that game, I thought grimly. I hadn't a doubt he was there. Common sense would have said, Wait till morning and ring Oxton, when I should probably hear that my son had returned the night before, but in circumstances like these common sense is always the loser. I mean, if you see your son playing with a rattle-snake I wouldn't think much of the mother who waited till she heard the rattles start before she picked up a cudgel and went in to do battle. These are the times when not having a car is such a nuisance. I had to wait for a Green Line coach from the main street, and going through Staines we got held up by a C.N.D. Rally. When I alighted I went into a nearby hotel and asked for a brandy and ginger ale and then inquired the way to Box-wood. The barman took for granted I had a car; when I heard it was two miles outside the village I wasn't surprised.

"Mr. Samson's place," he agreed chattily, bringing me my drink. "I did hear it was going up for sale. Well, no lady would want a place that size all to herself. Lonely, too, set in a cul-de-sac. All right for Mr. Samson, I daresay, but then he wasn't there much. Still," he added coolly, "they do say she had her friends."

Naturally there was no local bus, and even if I could have hired a car I wouldn't have done it. I wanted as little publicity about this visit as possible. All the way I was rehearsing what I was going to tell Madame, and there's no better way of making the miles and minutes fly. I missed my path once, but a stray traveler put me on the right road, and I began to walk down a long empty lane. Short of buying himself a location on a desert island, with a gull to bring the morning mail, I couldn't think of a more solitary environment Samson could have chosen. A Trappist monk would have been in his element there.

The house itself stood at the end of the lane, called Queen's Pikle, and was everything I would have expected it to be—florid and unimaginative and very, very expensive. For two people it was fantastic, there must have been ten rooms at least, plus attics and usual offices. The front garden had been laid out by someone with a footrule. I wasn't altogether certain at first that even the flowers weren't made of plastic. There were shutters at all the lower windows, which seemed reasonable when you remembered the isolation of the place and the fact that no sleeping-in servants were available —not that you could blame them. What I hadn't anticipated was that every shutter should be in place and fastened, and that there would be a printed card on the front door—No Milk Until Further Notice. Even in that moment of chagrin I found myself thinking, How typical that they'd have a printed card, where most of us just put a screw of paper in the mouth of a bottle. There were no newspapers on the step—but of course Annette might be like Miss Muir and not take a morning paper— but she must have gone off in too much of a hurry to warn the postman, because some envelopes were sticking out of the letter flap.

I stood disconsolately staring at the house, reflecting I'd now got to walk the two miles back, with no anticipatory conversation to sustain me. I might have been the only living creature for a mile around, I didn't even hear a dog bark or the whirr of a bird's wings. I rang the front-door bell, but naturally nothing happened. I pushed open the back gate and walked into a long not particularly well-kept garden leading to open common land. I wondered how long it would be before that was built over, detracting from the value of the house. But perhaps Samson had intended to buy it and do his own building. I don't quite know why I was so sure there'd be a swimming pool, but there wasn't one. I didn't linger there, no point, I thought, I didn't imagine they'd locked up the house and were wantoning in the woods.

No, Annette had gone all right, the question was, Had she gone alone? There was a big garage, firmly locked, and for good measure the small window was curtained. The whole place reeked with the abomination of desolation, but nothing changed my conviction that it was Annette who had sent the message. The question was why? And where could they be? I couldn't believe that the police had been in touch with Philip; Mall might be as intelligent as Crook seemed to suggest, but I'd given him no leads at all. Miss Muir would have said gleefully, "Perhaps they've Eloped!" but though I could credit almost any idiocy on the part of George's son, even I couldn't quite swallow that. I mean, what was there in it for Annette? Philip was a minor. Far more likely she was being blackmailed from another direction, and I suppose it would be second nature to her to expect someone else to get her out of the mess. She couldn't leave the country before the inquiry—at least I supposed she couldn't. I'd heard of people being asked to surrender their passports, I wondered if the police had hers.

I felt a proper fool hanging about around an empty house. I even wondered if it was all a trick to get me out of the way, only whose way? Well, I thought, this is where the mountain gets visited by Mahomet—or did I mean the other way around? At any events, let Crook earn his £200. I'd dumped the case in his lap, and if this wasn't a *cri de coeur,* if not precisely a message from on high, I don't know what could be. I'd tell him tonight, get his advice. I should look a bit silly if Philip turned up at Oxton in the morning, but I didn't like this latest development, I didn't like it one bit.

It was four o'clock when I returned, and Miss Muir came rushing to meet me from the garden square.

"You didn't tell me you were going out," she panted. "There's been a man . . ."

For an instant I thought of Philip, but, of course, she'd have recognized him.

"What sort of a man?" I asked. I opened my bag and was fumbling for my key. A handkerchief fluttered to the ground and Angela Muir stooped to pick it up.

"Oh, the usual," she said. "Two eyes and a nose. He said it was business."

"On a Sunday?"

"I did think it rather strange, but, of course, in your profession . . ."

"You make me sound like a streetwalker," I said, amazed to hear my voice emerge quite pleasant and cool.

"My dear, the things you say! Anyway, there aren't any now. These days they're all models."

"Did he ask for me by name?" I pursued.

"Of course. That's how I knew who he wanted. Anyway, it had to be one of us, and alas!" she puffed out a great, exaggerated sigh, "they're never for me, the fascinating strangers."

"Didn't he leave a name or anything?"

"He said he'd be back later. I don't think he was the press, though he did look a bit familiar. I mean, you can always tell, can't you? I told him I'd be around for the rest of the day, I'd keep an eye out for you—just in case you had any more engagements. My dear, you're looking Absolutely Drained. I'm sure you do too much. What's that handsome son of yours doing?"

"I wish I knew," I said. By this time we were in the hall.

"I do think a little Rest is called for." She smiled anxiously. I smiled back and held out my hand for the handkerchief. As she gave it to me a bit of paper fell out. Quick as a wink she had dived and rescued it, regardless of my Don't bother, it's only a bus ticket.

"Number seven-oh-two," she said brightly. "Isn't that the Virginia Water bus? I always used to go down by it when my sister was alive. She had a charming little house there." She fixed me with a round bright eye, like a cockyolly bird. "I don't know if you have any sisters, Mrs. Ross."

"Not any more," I said. What had made her mention Virginia Water rather than Staines, say? or Egham?

"Goodness, how sad. I can't imagine what it must be like to be a One Only—not that I think anyone need be sorry for Philip. I hope you have good news of him."

"It's a red-letter day when I have any news at all," I assured her. My upper lip was getting stiff with smiling. "Sometimes I wonder why we bother to teach our children to write."

"Ah yes," she said vaguely, "the telephone. Now, I have an idea. Why don't you come into my flat and let me make you a Nice Hot Cup of Tea?"

I wondered dispassionately what would happen if I put out my hand and covered her face and pushed. She had big indeterminate features, looking as though they were made of plasticine. It was Philip who said once, "I hope she's careful how she falls about. One feels she'd just flatten if she fell on her kisser."

I was a bit shocked to find this was the second person I'd wanted to obliterate in less than three days. And I remembered with surprise that Philip rather liked her. "She looks as if she'd been chipped off the Albert Memorial," he explained, "and you know what people say about that. We know it's awful, but can't imagine London without it." Stumbling up the stairs, having refused my neighbor's kind offer, it occurred to me suddenly that my unknown visitor might have been Crook, only surely even Miss Muir wouldn't have brushed him off so casually. My faint secret hope that I might find Philip waiting for me died when I let myself into my chilly-feeling flat. Anyway, hearing voices, he'd have come bounding out. Gregarious was his middle name. I felt I must talk to someone, and who was there except Crook, but as I put out my hand to pick up my receiver I remembered that ominous click I'd heard on the line while Roy was talking. By now I was convinced she wouldn't be above listening in if the conversation caught her fancy, and she didn't attempt to disguise her curiosity. And that pat mention of Virginia Water had shaken me. I admit that by now I was suspicious of practically everyone. I couldn't pass a policeman in the High Street without wondering if he had a concealed walkie-talkie set and was reporting on my movements. I even wondered if Miss Muir was in X's pay, and if you think that's melodramatic just wait till you're wearing my shoes.

I knew there was a phone box not far from the post office in the High Street, and although it was in huge demand during the week on a Sunday evening it might quite well be free. Anyway, it seemed my best bet. I pulled on a big loose coat and dug my hands into my pockets. I took a change purse and my latchkey and crept out onto the landing and listened. I suspected that Miss Muir was Ever Such a One for her tea, as she herself might put it. I waited another minute, then crept down my own stairs as surreptitiously as a thief.

I might have saved myself the trouble. As I opened the front door Miss Muir opened hers.

"Going out again, dear? Ho, we are restless. As a matter of fact, I was thinking about a bite myself. So, I thought, why not ask her to come in and share with me? What are neighbors for, and to be honest, dear, you look dead beat. Everything's at the ready, as a matter of fact, I was just going to beetle up and give the invitation in person. So absurd to use the telephone when we're both under the same roof."

I'd once been persuaded to have a meal with her, some exotic dish called Tortoise in the Hay or some such name, a variation on Toad in the Hole, she'd explained gaily, minced beef in place of sausages and a special kind of sauce.

"I'm going to the post, that's all," I said. "I shall have to hurry."

She looked at me in real dismay this time. "But, my dear, the post went out hours ago. There isn't a collection, even at the main office, after five-thirty on a Sunday."

"Well!" I looked at my watch. It still said four o'clock. "What is the time?" I asked. "My watch seems to have stopped."

"It's gone Seven," she told me.

I should have known. Naturally, I couldn't have made the double journey and done two long walks and lingered around the house and been home by four. Perhaps Philip was right, I was halfway to the nuthouse.

"It doesn't matter," I said. "I'll just pop it in the box." Her manner of talking was contagious. "Then it'll go out by the first collection, and seeing it's a London destination, it might be delivered in the afternoon."

"I'll just trot along with you," she offered obligingly. "I could do with a breather."

"Won't your Tortoise or whatever it is be spoiled?" I asked hopefully.

"It's cold chicken tonight. I buy joints at the supermarket; really it's as cheap as anything these days. When I was a gel . . ."

I could no more shake her off than you could shake a burr from a dog's coat. She came trotting beside me, wearing a heavy bright green golfer. "All this work," she chattered, "it's a mistake, it simply isn't true to say you can't have too much of a good thing. I always say health's the greatest treasure we possess." She branched off into some yarn about a friend who was nearly as rich as Midas but couldn't enjoy her money because she had polio of the brain.

"That's a new one on me," I said, willing her to fall off the pavement and split her skull. It sounded just the sort of thing I might be heading for, though. By this time I intended to get hold of Crook tonight, if I had to ring his alternate phone numbers from now till midnight. It was getting to a pretty pass, I told myself indignantly, when I couldn't even leave my own house without being shadowed. I remembered Crook's asking me if I thought I was being followed. Just let him ask again, I thought. He'd get the answer loud and clear.

The telephone box stood on the further side of the road opposite a public house called Robin in the Straw. There was a steady stream of London traffic dividing us from the opposite pavement. Suddenly I thought I saw a gap. If I could dive through that I'd be inside the box before Miss Dotty had a chance to cross, and even she wouldn't pull the door open once I'd started talking. I looked expertly this way and that, poised on the edge of the curb. There was a big gray car coming toward me. After that, I thought . . .

My feet were suddenly swept from under me, I threw up my hands in a perfectly futile gesture, I felt myself fall, something swept past me not more than four inches from my face, hot breaths nearly suffocated me. A man's voice yelled, "These bloody women!" Someone screamed.

I felt like a beetle lying on its back, trying to turn over before it can rise. I don't suppose my arms and legs were actually waving in the air, but that's what I felt they were doing. I opened my eyes cautiously, and that big rosy face loomed up like a cliff. Two hands started tugging at my shoulders, there was a babble of voices close by. Then one detached itself from the rest.

"Not that way, ma'am," it said. Two arms caught me under the shoulders, I was hoisted to my feet, a smiling dark-skinned face looked into mine.

"You are not hurt?" There was a warmth about the West Indian voice that seemed very strengthening, very composing. I wasn't aware of much sympathy flowing to me from any other direction. Miss Muir was chattering away like a leaky tap.

"My dear—what on earth . . . ? I warned you you were overdoing it. Couldn't you see the car?"

"Of course I saw the car," I replied shakily. "In fact, it's the last thing I ever expected to see." I looked around. "I notice it hasn't stopped. I suppose no one thought of taking its number."

"Well, dear, you couldn't really say it is the Driver's Fault," bleated Miss Muir.

"I suppose I deliberately threw myself under the wheels."

"Of course not. Still, to a stranger your behavior must have looked distinctly *odd*. Someone who didn't realize the Strain you've been under." She turned to the West Indian, whose girl waited impatiently near by. "Thank you for helping my friend up," she said. "She slipped, a slight attack of vertigo, she's been Overdoing It."

"You will be okay now?" he asked.

I wanted to yell no, but Miss Muir told him easily, "Of course." And there was no necessity for him to offer to see us home, she was perfectly capable, nursing experience . . .

"Why didn't that car stop?" I demanded as the West Indian moved off.

"He didn't actually hit you—he must have been a very good driver to have avoided you, you know."

"He should have stopped anyway," I insisted.

"Perhaps he couldn't, perhaps he was a doctor going to Save a Life."

"And take mine by the way. That cancels out." I was more shaken than I wanted her to guess.

"My dear, you seemed to lose your head completely. You suddenly turned around and darted across the road. Or tried to."

I said, "My phone's out of order. I wanted to report it."

"As if I wouldn't have done that for you! Or you could have used mine, that's working all right. Now, I suggest you just sit down here." She indicated the Robin bar. "Here's a table near the door, the air, you know, have a little shot of brandy . . ." A tall young woman in skin-tight white slacks and a black turtleneck sweater said in audible tones, "Wouldn't black coffee be more to the point?"

Miss Muir turned like an avenging fury. "Nonsense. My friend has been out all day, only just got back, she is Quite exhausted. Give me your letter, dear," she turned to me with a paralyzing smile, "and I'll post it while you're waiting for the brandy." She beckoned to a waiter.

"Bank Holiday in the bin," said the girl in white slacks. I wished she'd stop talking. I supposed I must have struck my head when I fell; it seemed a perfectly natural thing to pick up one of the heavy china ashtrays and crown her with it.

"Your letter, dear," insisted Miss Muir.

I made a feint of feeling in my pockets. "I must have dropped it when I was knocked down," I said feebly.

Naturally she rushed to the door and looked up and down the street. "There's no sign of it," she reported.

"And I must confess, when I met you in the hall you weren't carrying anything in your hand."

"Had it in my pocket," I insisted.

"I daresay you thought you had. You'll probably find it on the table when you get back. It's terrible how absent-minded we girls can be. Well, I'll just pop over and report your telephone." And off she dodged, looking like an aged Puck.

The waiter brought the brandy and stood beside the table. I fished out my purse, but I'd only brought sufficient for the phone call. "You must wait for my companion to come back," I said. "She'll be wanting something."

Miss Muir had shut herself into the box and seemed to be jabbering away nineteen to the dozen. She wasn't reporting my imaginary trouble, I wasn't fool enough to believe that, she was sending a message to Assailants Anonymous. "Didn't quite manage it," she'd be saying in her bright way, "but there's always tomorrow."

When she came back she announced, beaming, to anyone who was interested, "They've rung your number, dear, they say there's nothing wrong."

The waiter came back. "Have one on me," I said. "I'll settle with you when we get back."

Miss Muir hauled a little zip purse out of her pocket. It was bright green leather stamped with gold stars. "Florence!" she announced, taking out some money and giving it to the waiter.

A big red-faced chap, who must have completed his first lap at home, leaned forward and said, "Have one on me, Florence."

"If you're addressing me, sir," said Miss Muir, "my name is Angela."

"Angel of light," said the drunken fool. "Singing to welcome the pilgrims of the night."

"For God's sake!" I said, downing my brandy. "No,

it's all right, thank you. I'm perfectly capable of walking unaided."

"That's what you think," said White Slacks.

Miss Muir startled me by saying cozily, "It's never wise to judge others by yourself," and I had the dubious satisfaction of hearing another chuckle go up, this time not at my expense.

After that I made no attempt to get in touch with Crook, not that evening. I'd shake off my incubus somehow in the morning, go and see him in person, that would be the best way. I hung about in my flat till midnight, hoping against hope the phone would ring, but it never gave a tinkle. I was a bit surprised Miss Muir didn't come through again. In a sudden burst of optimism I decided she'd had a stroke and was lying helpless on the hearth rug. Then I asked myself why I should expect miracles to be performed for me. I took two red sleeping pills, which is twice what the doctor recommends, locked my flat door with the mortice, a thing I never do in the ordinary way, and collapsed into bed.

X

It is amazing what sleep and the coming of a new day will do. In the morning I felt a surge of resilience, a damping-down of the doubts of last night. I would ring Oxton and find that Philip had returned, he had simply been down to help Annette close Boxwood and see her established elsewhere. My notion that someone had tried to run me down outside Robin in the Straw was fantastic. I had chosen my moment ill, had misjudged the distance between me and the gray car. Miss Muir was simply the Christmas-card figure she appeared. I was absolutely amazed that I should have allowed myself to get into such a stew.

Everyone must have seen a morning, quite early, even in a city, when the snow lies smooth and white. Not a footfall, not a smear, a carpet of beauty. And within the hour it's just a mess of mud, footprints, wheel tracks, gravel, brown slime that stains your stockings. It was like that with me. First of all, was the phone message. I had just heard the front door close and rushed to the window to see Miss Muir going out with a shopping basket big enough to conceal a baby. This seemed my opportunity. I picked up the phone and dialed Philip's rooms in Oxton. A slatternly voice, the sort that goes with curlers at the breakfast table, answered me.

"Mr. Ross? Naow, 'e's not 'ere. Gone to London. You a friend of 'is?"

"You could say that."

An obscene throaty chuckle gurgled down the line. "It's 'is mum, see. Right round the bend. Ever so sad really. 'E's 'ad to go to London. No, I couldn't say when 'e'll be back. If you like to leave a name . . ." I could see the leer as clearly as though this were a television confrontation.

I hung up. There was one illusion down the drain. I drank my coffee and ran my bath and noticed with surprise that it was already nine-thirty. I decided my best plan was to call a taxi while Little Red Riding Hood was out and drive up to Bloomsbury Street. I reminded myself that every taxi driver in London couldn't be in X's pay, and repeated firmly my conviction that last night was simply a coincidence. Surely, I told myself, it was odd that no one, but no one, had attempted to censure the driver. I was dressed and actually going toward the telephone when the front-door bell rang. I looked out of the window. The disadvantage of these automatic porters is that you can't see your visitor, and if he announces himself as the man come to read the meter and then comes beetling up the stairs with a dirk between his teeth there's very little you can do about it. A tall fair man was standing patiently on the step. At the sound of my window opening he lifted his head, and it was Mark Spurr.

"I'll let you in," I called. I didn't know why he'd come. At all events he'd gained his liberty, so I'd done that much for him. The only reason I could imagine he was here was to talk some more about the letter.

"I hope I'm not too early," he apologized in an odd formal voice.

"On the contrary, you've just caught me. Another five minutes and I'd have gone."

"The fate of empires has been decided in less. Mrs. Ross, I've come to ask you to help me, if you can. You can guess what it's about."

"The letter?" I hazarded.

"Yes. I know you told the police that the envelope you showed us is the one you found in Samson's room."

"It's the truth. I can't change that."

"I suppose that's what I should have anticipated. I had a sort of wild hope you might have substituted the envelope; having been in Samson's power yourself, you'd know what danger means."

"I didn't," I said. "In fact, on the whole I seem to have done you a bad turn. If I'd left the envelope where it was you'd never have been suspected at all. When did they release you?" I added.

He smiled wryly. "More to the point, why. It seems that more people know Tom Fool than Tom Fool knows. I fancy someone pulled a string, anyway that's the impression I got. Not that it's really freedom, only a sort of parole. Perhaps they think, Give him enough rope and this time he'll really hang himself." There was a cynical bitterness in his voice that contrasted oddly with his easy-going appearance. He looked about him. "This is a friendly room," he said.

"Even Samson discovered that."

He looked startled. "You mean he came *here?*"

"To let me know his terms. At first I couldn't place him . . ."

Mark Spurr nodded. "It is a shock to find you're being blackmailed. No," he corrected himself, "to find you're in a position where you *can* be blackmailed. Mrs. Ross, that envelope . . ."

"You're as bad as the police," I cried. "They didn't believe me either."

He walked about the room, even smiting his forehead in what struck me as a slightly theatrical manner. He stopped in front of one or two pictures, but I'd swear he never saw them.

"Of course I believe you," he said. "It's just that hope dies hard. At least I knew who my master was, Samson was bad enough . . ."

"I can't imagine why no one had killed him before this," I burst out.

My companion pulled a wry mouth. "It all goes to show that some people do get their deserts, if a bit late for some of us. He must have lived on tenterhooks all the same, having that gun handy and letting everyone who came to see him know he had it. *And* would have used it."

"But he didn't. My lawyer says if we knew why, we'd be halfway to the solution. I think it's because the man who killed him was someone he held in absolute contempt. Mr. Crook says that's always dangerous. Unless, of course, he only kept it as a threat and never intended to use it."

"He'd have used it all right," said Mark grimly. (It was sometime during this conversation that I found we'd slipped into first names; I suppose you can't have many closer links with someone than being co-victims of a blackmailer.) "Only I never believed he'd need to. It takes more courage than the average man possesses to walk straight up to a gun that's being leveled at your heart."

"He'd have to explain the body away, though."

"Protecting his own property. The law permits that. He kept a lot of cash on the premises, or didn't you know?"

"I never contributed any."

His head came up sharply. "That's another link between us. Amateurs always assume that payment has to be in cash; sometimes it's in kind."

"Mine would have been cash if I could have raised it, or needed to, but in the circumstances someone else made that unnecessary."

"I suppose by that time he thought of himself as invulnerable. He'd been manipulating other men's lives for so long. You know, I can't help wondering what he had on you. You don't look the type . . ."

"Is there a type?" I asked. "Isn't it more that most of us are fools but some of us are unlucky. I happen to have a son," I added. "I'd do anything, short of murder, to protect him."

Mark looked at me in perplexity. "And yet you went to the police—you weren't suspect, were you?"

"Why should I be? There was nothing on the premises to connect me with Samson."

"Which makes it all the more difficult to understand . . ."

"But I knew you hadn't done it," I protested. "I was there when you phoned and Samson was already dead."

"Did no one ever tell you that self-preservation is the first law?"

"I told you I'd do anything short of murder for my son. If I'd kept quiet and the case had gone against you, I'd have felt on a par with whoever is really responsible. It seems to me it must have been the one who came in before me," I added. "If the police could discover who that was." I paused. "If he's the one who took your envelope," I said, "you're likely to be the one to answer that question."

"Why mine?" he demanded. "Why mine? Oh, there's some trickery here. He didn't take yours."

"I couldn't be of any conceivable use to him."

"And you think I could?" he stopped. "That could

be the answer. Did you ever wonder how I came under Samson's thumb?"

"I thought perhaps you were a doctor . . ."

He half smiled, but there was no amusement there. "Performing illegal abortions or giving mercy drugs out of pure pity? Nothing so high-minded, I'm afraid. I'm an inquiry agent."

"I thought they only existed in novels."

"Who do you suppose amasses the evidence in legal cases?"

"Divorce and all that?"

"Particularly all that. It's another face of justice, you know. Innocence by itself can be remarkably helpless."

"And—something went wrong?"

"Isn't it always the same story? You get into a bit of trouble, as a flyer may suddenly get into a pocket of air. You've got to get out double quick if you're not going to crash, so you take chances you wouldn't think of taking in the ordinary way. On the surface, it didn't seem so bad. I'd been making an inquiry and I'd uncovered a name. The owner of the name was prepared to get me out of my difficulties if I'd forget I'd ever heard it. As simple as that. And it wouldn't really make any difference, there were so many names."

"So you did?"

"There was no reason to suppose I'd ever unearthed the name, but unfortunately I was challenged—on oath. I had a split second in which to make up my mind and I chose wrong. It's always easy to say that afterwards."

"And Samson found out? Could he act?"

He looked at me oddly. "You don't know much about perjury, do you? It's an indictable offense."

"And that's what you'd committed? Could Samson have proved it?"

"Unfortunately there were documents. Now you see

why it's so important for me to know who has them now."

I said slowly, "There's something that's occurred to me, thinking about the case. How do men like Samson ever accumulate enough evidence to start a blackmail racket? Or is it a thing that snowballs? You might find one victim, but one swallow doesn't make a summer."

"They follow the example of the police," Mark told me. "They have their informants who fill in the gaps or even pass the original word. Samson would have his. I told you some people paid by kind."

I gave an involuntary shiver. It couldn't be a nice thought, that you'd been working with a louse like Samson. "Have you got a family?" I asked involuntarily.

"I had a fiancée once, but she changed her mind. After I got entangled with Samson, I was hardly in a position to make ties—if it had just been money there could have been a way out. I can't tell you how often I thought that if I could be sure of not being identified, I'd destroy him myself."

"If he had you in his power like this," I said slowly, "there must have been others. If he kept any sort of record—but of course he did. The card index. One of those names must be the man the police are looking for."

"We can't even be certain of that. He might have taken the one step too far that blackmailers often do, tried to twist the arm of a man who wasn't prepared to meet his demands. Your name wasn't on a card, perhaps this man's wasn't either."

"A new name?" I brooded. "But wouldn't he be particularly on guard against someone he didn't know?"

"There comes a time when men have been successful —oh, in a very mean way, I admit, but it's success in their line—been successful for so long they come to think of themselves as invulnerable. They get careless, and that's when X strikes."

"Or—you've just said a racket like this can't be run singlehanded. He might have a partner who threatened to sell him down the river, someone who could, if need be, go to the police. I mean, it's not like a husband and wife who can't testify against each other—at least, the police take a pretty poor view of it if they do . . ." I stopped hearing my own words come echoing back through that quiet room. It was a dull day, the air gray and the leaves on the trees outside practically motionless. Later on there would be a storm. "Oh no," I heard that unfamiliar voice whisper. "It couldn't have been that."

"If you're going to faint," said Mark, and his voice seemed to come from behind glass, "put your head between your knees. Do you have any brandy or anything on the premises?"

"I don't want any brandy," I said. "Listen. Annette used to go to Maygate Street, did the occasional letter, I daresay set the scene, dug out the appropriate envelopes, you know. I always realized he didn't marry her just for her looks, though they're an asset enough. She knew too much, and only a wife—that is, she'd only be safe from his point of view if she was his wife. And she likes her comforts, her high-couture clothes— if he was out of the way she'd be a rich widow."

"We don't know that," said Mark, sharply. "You're riding well ahead of the hounds."

"He put a lot of his securities in her name as a kind of insurance. She told me that herself. He wouldn't have done it if she hadn't been pretty useful to him."

"The decoy duck, in short. That's the oldest trick in the book. Could she do it?"

For answer I pulled open the drawer of my writing desk and rummaged out my postcard album. I found my picture of Jacopo's Child with Guitar. "That gives you a pretty good idea," I said.

Mark just stared. "But that's a child."

"That's probably what she counts on." The sound of thunder that had been roaring in my ears died down, the dust began to settle. "It adds up," I insisted. "However improbable it seems, she's the one person who could have engineered this. She'd know about you, she may even intend to carry on her husband's racket, you'd be invaluable then."

Mark had been thinking. "There's something here I don't understand. I thought you'd only seen Samson that once. He came alone?"

"Of course."

"And you only went that once to the office?"

"So how do I know what Annette looks like? I'll tell you. Because she came here. Oh, what's the use of playing it cagey? Crook knows, presently everyone will know. The letters were written by my son, Philip . . ."

"To Mrs. Samson?"

"You've seen her picture," I said simply.

"But—he's only a boy. She can't have thought anything serious could come of it."

"She wasn't out for anything serious, she was simply out for money."

His glance went around my room. Hardly a millionairess' apartment, you'd say.

"My son gave her the impression that he had a wealthy father vegetating in the Lakes. She must have thought she had it made. Oh, she's got him, hook, line and sinker. She said she wanted to go on the stage," I recalled. "The stage has missed something when she became Mrs. Alfred Samson instead."

Because the truly appalling thought had struck me that on her side the whole thing had been as cold-blooded as a refrigerator. If she suddenly decided to take the huge risk of being party to a murder plot, it seemed to me she could have only one reason, another man and this time someone permanent. The idea that she could have used Philip as a screen to deflect her husband's suspicions made me cry out, "I wish I'd killed her, I wish I'd killed her."

"There's been altogether too much killing already," observed Mark in a dry voice. "All this is supposition anyway."

"Two and two make four," I said.

"That's one of the things we're taught at school, but it doesn't always work out. Who was the chap who said they sometimes made ninety-six? Chesterton?"

"It sounds like him," I agreed. "She put the card right into my hand," I marveled. "She said the incriminating photograph that was the beginning of this nightmare for me could have been engineered by her husband. It would be even simpler if it had been engineered by the pair of them working as a team. You see where that gets us?"

"You're like the young lady called Bright whose movements were faster than light. No, I'm not sure I do."

"It means she knows who did the murder. Oh, she won't be personally involved. I wondered if there was anything wrong with her car that night. That's her alibi, you see, that she had to take it to a garage at a time that would exonerate her completely. But if she'd come as usual to Maygate Street to set the scene, don't you see, that would give her the opportunity to swap envelopes. Why, yours may not be the only one. And that creature was on the premises when I arrived."

"You're in the clear," Mark assured me. "You've been to the police—do they know about the letters?"

"Not from me. Not that Philip wrote them, I mean. I don't see why they should. Annette won't tell, the letters are destroyed . . ."

"There's still your son. He could be a source of danger."

It was terrible to reflect that while I was talking to Mark my son's danger had taken a back place in my mind. With his words another piece of the puzzle—a large one this time—fell into place.

"She's not so stupid she won't have appreciated that. Of course, that explains the message. Philip's disappeared," I added impatiently. I told him about the phone call, and my visit to Virginia Water the previous day. "If we're right—oh, I admit it's all speculation, but when you start building you have to put down your foundations somewhere—she won't take chances. Her husband's out of the way, you're being held for the murder—does she know you're free?"

"Well, not from me, of course, but if she has an accomplice he's probably covering all the lines."

"Still, you don't really know anything, do you? Philip's different. He could be in mortal danger."

"Not only Philip," said Mark quietly. "Not once the opposition realizes you're on the right track."

I put my hand to my forehead. It was like those Chinese boxes, every time you remove one you find yet another inside, and you go on practically to infinity.

"Perhaps it wasn't coincidence, after all," I said, forgetting he didn't know about my slip-up outside the Robin in the Straw. I told him. I have to admit he looked a bit skeptical. "How did anyone know you were going to be there?"

"Only if they've got a spy watching me."

He got my meaning at once. "The old lady downstairs? I have to admit, Margaret, it doesn't seem very probable."

"She knew I'd been to Virginia Water."

"A bow at a venture?"

"Perhaps. But perhaps not."

164

"Had you said anything to give her a clue?" His sharp eyes roamed round the room. "You have a party line," he discovered. "Would she . . . ?"

"Listen in? I wouldn't be a bit surprised. Mark, suppose we're looking through the wrong end of the telescope? Suppose someone told her I'd been there?"

"You said the house was closed."

"That's what I was meant to think."

"But what was the idea . . . ?"

"I'm not sure," I said, "but I'm going down there again right away, and this time I won't give her a chance of getting in first, if I have to cut off Miss Muir's head with my own bread knife."

"I still think you're barking up the wrong tree. Where's the sense in this woman giving the impression she's gone away? The police aren't after her; she'd know she couldn't go abroad, at least I should imagine not; there are a score of places she could be, a private hotel, a furnished apartment, or she could be staying incognito at Torquay or John o' Groats . . ."

"It's not Annette's whereabouts that interest me," I told him clearly and slowly. "It's my son. I'll tell you something else. When I asked the barman the whereabouts of Boxwood he didn't say, Oh the house is empty, you won't find anyone at home. And nor did the passer-by I asked when I missed the way. And why? Because neither of them knew. She hadn't informed the postman and anyone can put out a note for the milk."

At this juncture Mark reminded me more than ever of George at his own most obstructive, the same slow reasoning from point to point, like some old ram nosing its way up the mountainside, with me leaping ahead almost out of sight, like some inspired chamois.

"If she's still there she's got to get provisions somehow . . ." he began.

"I didn't say she was there," I howled. "I said it's possible that Philip is."

Even then he didn't leap to it. "If the place is locked up, how do you propose to get in? Or were you thinking of taking the police with you?"

"The police!" I almost spat. "The police act on information received and crimes committed. I haven't a ha'porth of evidence, as you're so laboriously pointing out. Even Mr. Crook wouldn't break into a house on such a fragile web of suspicion."

"Break in?" It was like having a puzzled but docile parrot in the room.

"If I have to go down the chimney. I'm not bad as a housebreaker," I added. "That's the best of having a youthful son, they do teach you a lot of wrinkles."

"If you're in earnest about this," Mark said, "of course I shall come with you. I suppose you do realize you're running head-on into danger?"

"You see?" I cried. "You have your suspicions, too."

I was remembering that silent house and the sinister grounds stretching away to heaven knows where. I found myself recalling the Forest of Gambais where Landru interred so many victims whose bodies were never recovered.

"I think I'll have that brandy now," I said sharply. "You'd better have one, too."

He brought it—he was very neat-handed, observant, too. I thought he'd be a good ally to take with me on what I suppose you might call a fact-finding expedition. Because, as I explained to him, I didn't necessarily anticipate finding Philip on the premises, it would be too obvious, one of the first places the police would look when they knew the truth about the letters and the phone message—but if I could give them some proof that he'd been there. I didn't trust anyone to get to work with my expedition, I was the most interested party by about a thousand miles. A thousand? A million.

"There's one other consideration you should take into mind," Mark was saying in his rational way. "Annette doesn't sound any fool, she may know you'll go straight down to Boxwood."

"Then why didn't she tackle me yesterday?"

He nodded. "You have a point there. All the same, with your permission, I'll come with you. It'll be much quicker in my car anyway. And even a ghoul like Annette can't go on slaying to infinity. Always assuming this isn't a sheer fabrication and she's not mixed up in this at all."

"Of course she's mixed up in this," I told him contemptuously. "Who else would have sent that message?" I looked at the clock. I was amazed to see how late it was. Time was like one of those tides you find in Brittany, that come racing up like horses, faster than a man can run. Philip and I had almost got caught once and crawled out dripping to the waist; and if my son thought it all rather a lark, I was frightened nearly to death.

"One more thing," I said. "I may be doing her an injustice, but I would like to immobilize Miss Muir just for the next few hours. If one could give her the impression we were going to the pictures or something . . ."

"Didn't you say she has the party line? Well, if she listens in, here's her opportunity. Get your hat, Margaret, if 'twere done 'twere well 'twere done quickly. How complicated the Middle Ages made the English language."

Changing into a tweed suit that would look more suitable for a drive into the country, putting on low-heeled shoes, tying up my hair in my Italian silk scarf, I could hear him talking on the phone.

"The Burgoyne?" he said. "We should like a table

for two for twelve-thirty." He gave my name, partly, he explained, to wrap it up for Miss Muir, and also because he didn't want the smallest chance of being identified with the Spurr whose picture had been in all the papers and who was still, in a good many minds, first suspect for Alfred Samson's murder. He pulled out a cigarette and a very elegantly monogrammed lighter.

"Just one to calm the nerves," he said. "And take a leaf out of Miss Muir's book."

When we were alight he noiselessly lifted the receiver, listened, then gently put it back.

"She's not passing on the information, at all events not so long as we're in the flat," he said.

"Was she listening?"

"I don't know. But I daresay we soon shall."

Sure enough, as we came down the stairs her door opened, and out she popped, wearing a sort of gold snood around her head and carrying an open-work gold string bag containing a paperback and a bulky purse.

"Going out?" she asked gaily. "Don't I recognize your friend? Of course, the one who called yesterday. I'm so glad you didn't make a second journey for nothing. I always say we get too little good weather to waste it indoors." She patted the gold bag. "I'm off to the park, the Riverside Café, you know, quite continental, right on the edge of the water. I think sometimes if this were Paris instead of despised old London we should all hold our breath at the beauty of that view from the bridge. It's a case, I'm afraid, of familiarity breeding contempt. Do you know"—she pulled on a pair of fabric gloves—"the Chinese geese had a family this year."

"Fascinating!" I applauded.

"And there's the man who brings the monkey for a run, the sweetest little thing, the monkey, I mean. Follows him like a dog, except, naturally, when it runs up trees . . ."

"So we shan't be seeing you at the Burgoyne," I said clearly.

She laughed so heartily the ceiling nearly fell down. They're never very stable in these old houses. "Joke bomb!" she panted. "Who'd pay for my lunch at a place like the Burgoyne. No, I shall have a salad sandwich, they cut a French loaf longwise, quite delicious."

"Did you see about the man who saw a puffin walking up the Strand?" inquired Mark, playing the ball back into her court.

She looked delighted. " 'All human life is there,' " she quoted. "And better than human when you come to think of it. That's a lovely scarf you're wearing, dear. It seems to bring Venice right into the room. Still, not to be envious. Marks and Sparks offers the most wonderful selection."

She clattered down the steps in front of us when Mark opened the door. He had left his car outside, a Philomel it was. "I've no right to run a car this size," he acknowledged a little guiltily, "but you don't get much for them second-hand and I do like some room when I'm driving." Again like George, he was the long-legged type. As he put her into gear and we shot away, he said, "That old girl, she's like an aged bunny. Can't ever have a dull moment with her on the premises. Can't you just see her, feeding the Chinese geese, blowing kisses to the monkey . . ." But I wasn't amused. All I could see was my son in mortal danger.

Even in a car like the Philomel it was a frustrating ride. It was Market Day apparently, at all events the stalls were out, and then we got jammed behind a huge British Railways truck, that in its turn was halted by its twin brother racing it across a crossroads. But at last Mark turned off the main road, he said he knew a short cut. The day's humidity had increased, the clouds hung low, tinged with violet that would presently turn to a grape-bloom purple. The thunder went racketing through my head, though there wasn't so much as a rumble of it in the sky. I felt my heart clanging and my hands were sticky. The road here was unfamiliar, but whatever qualities Mark didn't possess he clearly had a sense of direction. We reached the entrance to the Pikle before I realized we were approaching it, and went sailing down.

At the end the house stood, blank as an idiot, quiet as the long-dead.

XI

The only difference between Boxwood today and the same house yesterday was that the notice about the milk hung a little crooked, but the wind would account for that. It had been quite stormy during the night. I thought there were a few more envelopes in the letter box, I supposed the postman would go on delivering until someone told him to stop.

Mark came up beside me. He had parked the car a short way up the lane, in case someone was at home and saw it. But he needn't have bothered.

"Convinced?" he murmured.

"I still intend to get in."

I pushed open the back gate and walked into the garden. It was odd that so little trouble had been taken here, or perhaps Samson had been planning to have the whole returfed. It occurred to me I didn't know how long he had been living here. I looked around me. I don't quite know what I expected to see—Annette hanging from the branches? Not likely, anyhow not since yesterday. In any case, sleeping pills would be more like her. Everything around me seemed even stiller than before. I stared out at a fringe of poplars against the sky, skinny-looking trees, I thought, remembering great avenues of them on the Continent. The soil didn't suit them perhaps.

It had been one of those steely mornings when you wait for something to happen. Now suddenly the face of nature quickened, as though our coming had been a signal. The branches of all the shrubs and the few trees started to sway wildly in a storm of wind that had sprung up from nowhere, from behind the dun skies a white radiance emerged, and the pale clouds started to turn. You could actually watch them doing it, darker and darker until they were almost black. There was a terrible beauty about them that I'd noticed before prior to the breaking storm. There was an electricity in the air, too, it thrummed like a wire. At any minute now the climax would come, the skies would split with the force of a tornado. I knew it was ridiculous to stay in the garden, in thirty seconds you could get soaked to the skin. I threw one last despairing glance around me, looking, I suppose, for some weak place where I could break into the house; it was then that my eye caught the shine of something in the rock-edged borders under the window. It was nothing very startling, only some pieces of broken glass, a milk bottle, I supposed, though it seemed an odd place to find them. When I went nearer I saw it wasn't bottle glass, the pieces were too large, not convex. I looked up sharply and saw that a pane in an upper window had been broken, one of the attics that probably no one used.

Mark's gaze followed mine. "Typical," he murmured. "Probably everything like an exhibition inside the house, but up at the top—that window may have been broken for ages."

"No," I said. "Glass that's been lying about for any length of time gets dirty, particularly when it's in contact with earth." I felt like a professor, or as I suppose a professor might feel, giving instruction to an unobservant class. "That break's quite new. But why the attics?" I knew a sudden frenzy of activity. "Quick," I said, "before the storm breaks."

"Was it there yesterday?" Mark said; his train of thought was clearly following mine.

"I don't know. I didn't really look, and anyway I was so disappointed, so agitated, to find the house shut, there could have been a lion lurking in the shrubbery and I wouldn't have noticed."

Only, of course, that wasn't true. One of the things that had impressed me so much was the absence of any movement or any indication of life.

"I suppose it could have been broken by a child's ball," suggested Mark idiotically. No child, even if there'd been one near by, could have tossed a ball to that height.

"There must be some way of getting in," I said. There was the usual narrow window opening outward, with starred glass, a downstairs cloakroom they'd call that, but even Miss Muir's monkey would have had a job to make an entry that way. Either the front or back door must have been used by whoever locked the shutters, when he (she?) made a getaway. I caught the handle of the back door and shook it hard.

"This isn't bolted on the inside," I said. I dropped down and looked through the keyhole. I could see clear into the passage. X had gone out, fastened the door and removed the key. It's an ordinary enough proceeding in these days when houses have to be left empty and there are a lot of rogues about. The usual thing is to hide the key under a stone or hang it on a concealed nail. I started looking frantically, but there was no sign. This, to me, was conclusive evidence that X didn't intend to return. That was what Crook would call female logic, which, he declared, the sex spelled Intuition.

"Have you got a knife?" I said. "We might be able to get this door open. Philip's showed me how, if you get locked out of your flat," I explained. "But you need a knife." There was a tool shed on the corner, but that was locked, too, and there was the garage. Surely, I said, there'll be something there we can use. I hauled off a shoe and slammed it through the glass window.

"Take care you don't cut yourself," said Mark sharply. I pulled off my scarf and wound it around my wrist. For the first time luck favored us. Just under the window was a narrow shelf with various tools lying along it. It wasn't at the shelf that I was staring, though.

"The sooner we get that house open the better," I told Mark. "Annette doesn't strike me as the sort of girl who'd walk two miles to the main road, and however she went, it wasn't by car, because her car's still in the garage." I stared at it for a minute, the big light-blue body that I'd last seen standing outside my London flat.

"What we want's a locksmith," said Mark, looking around as if he expected one to fall out of a tree.

"A locksmith might make a neater job of it," I agreed, "but we haven't the time. It's as dark as the inside of Jonah's whale in the garage, can't you put on your lighter?"

He snapped on the little flame and we could see a chisel nearby. "Is that any use?" he said.

"It'll be too thick. What we want is a knife. And a hammer if we can find one. You have to hammer the blade between the door and the jamb till you engage the lock, then you can push it back. Oh, you must have seen men put in a new sashcord, it's the same principle." In my impatience I joggled against him and the lighter slipped out of his hand to the garage floor. "Never mind," I told him, "there's one in my bag." I had put it down beside the door, and I ran and fetched it. Half the time my lighter doesn't work, but today, for a miracle, it went on at once. And beyond the chisel, like a reward for a bright boy, I saw both a hammer and a knife. For an instant I really didn't believe my eyes, but they were real enough. I hauled them both out and got to work. The noise of the hammer was startling, breaking up the silence as though it were glass. Every moment the sky darkened; now it was like being in twilight.

"Hold the light nearer," I told Mark. I caught a glimpse of his face. He thought I had gone mad. I daresay I did look like the mother of the Wizard of Oz, but who cares? From a tree behind me a jay began to call; we have one in our London garden sometimes, they have the most discordant voices of any bird I know, and I always associate them with ill luck. This one seemed to be screaming hoarse gibes at me. "Can't you throw something at it?" I demanded, almost beside myself.

"Do you really expect to get that door open?" asked Mark in awe-struck tones.

"I bet Crook could do this at the drop of a hat," I told him. I couldn't think why I'd brought along anyone so helpless. Even George would have shown more gumption. Still, George was in New Zealand, no good thinking about him. They talk about time standing still, it didn't stand still for me, it tore past, every second striking its own death knell.

"Wait a minute," I panted suddenly. "I almost had it then." I'd abandoned the hammer, and now the blade of the knife was feeling delicately this way and that. At the same time you have to keep hold of the door handle, and directly the lock seemed to give a fraction, you shove. It's helpful on occasions like these to have three hands.

"Let me take it now," Mark offered, but I pushed him away. Amateurs can break a blade, and that knife was all we had. I had two more near-misses and then the door was open and I was flung into the passage. Every door around me was closed, the house was fantastically dark, but whoever had staged this melodrama had either forgotten about switching off the light at the main or hadn't thought it necessary. Anyhow, when I depressed the nearest switch the light came on. The inside was a hotchpotch, hand-painted china finger plates and door handles that didn't accord in the least with the doors themselves, all of which were locked on the outside. But the keys were in place. I turned the first one automatically, put on the light there too—emptiness.

The body was behind the third door I opened. In my heart I realized that this was what I had been anticipating. I almost fell over it, and as the light sprang up, the storm broke. It felt like the end of the world. Thunder roared through the sky like forty jets at once, lightning flashed, the rain fell as if the world had turned turtle and the whole sea crashed down upon us. I heard a crack as a branch gave, and the jay yelled its defiance or its terror and was still. I was aware of Mark's arm around my shoulders. I was babbling.

"It's not fair," I said. "You couldn't expect anyone to look like Jacopo's child after that treatment."

I felt his hand come up behind my head, he pressed my eyes against his shoulder. "Don't look," he told me.

No one can retain much beauty when a gun has been fired at point-blank range; anyway, Annette had none. As I moved, my foot struck something and I wrenched myself free and stooped to pick it up from the floor. It nestled into my hand as comfortably as a glove you have been wearing for weeks.

Mark's voice came to me sharply. "What's that?

Margaret, you shouldn't have touched it. Didn't you ever hear about fingerprints?"

"It must have had mine on it for years," I said stupidly. I was trying to do my mental arithmetic. Two and two make—what? Four? Ninety-six? A hundred and ninety-six perhaps. The problem that irked me was why my gun, taken from my flat by my son, should be lying by Annette's body. When had he given it to her? Was that why he'd arrived at Oxton so late that Monday night, because in spite of her promise, she'd met him, and he'd given it to her for her protection? Or had he brought it down with him on Friday? Something that sounded like a dozen jays clamored in the room.

"Don't laugh," I cried fiercely, "it's not amusing." Only in a diabolical way it was. "It's becoming quite a habit, finding bodies in strange surroundings."

Mark literally pulled me out of the room. I must have dropped the pistol somewhere, I never heard it fall. I sat on a stair and my eye caught a small white object lying on the hall table. "What's that?" I said, but he had disappeared to get me some water or something, so I staggered to my feet and collected it myself. It was a visiting card inscribed Mr. Maxwell Price and an address in Outer London.

"Who's Price?" I inquired.

"Let the police deal with that one." Mark was back at my side. "Here. I can't find any brandy, there's only whiskey." He put a little glass into my hand. Like a water diviner, I thought, only it's not water. I hate whiskey, even the smell is enough to turn my stomach.

"Oh, drink it," said Mark impatiently.

I took the glass and balanced it on my knee. "If he brought it down on Friday," I said, "how is it she's the one who was shot? She was shot, wasn't she?" I looked up. "Where's that gun? I want it."

"It's police evidence," insisted Mark.

"You're very fussy about the police all of a sudden," I sneered.

"I don't think you've got the measure of the situation," Mark told me. "I suppose it's right, you do recognize your own weapon?"

"Of course it's mine," I said. "It's also what the police will call the murder weapon."

"And you were down here yesterday. Of course, I don't know how long she's been there . . ."

"I didn't get in yesterday," I said. "You know I didn't."

"I know you said you didn't, and I believe you, but will the police? You've told me no one knew the house was closed, not the locals, I mean, and whoever shot that woman, she didn't do it herself."

I became aware again of the power of the storm. For a minute it seemed to paralyze thought, then I understood he was telling me I might be accused of shooting Annette. It was ridiculous, even a blockhead of a policeman couldn't think that. But I could have come down, broken in or been admitted by Annette, accused her of using my son as a decoy—but no, I hadn't thought about that yesterday, had I? Still, I had plenty against her without that—and I could have turned the pistol on her, and gone around closing the house.

"I wouldn't know about the milk notice," I said. I'd heard that in moments of crisis it's the trifles that occupy the mind.

Mark went into the room of death, as the press were certainly going to call it, and brought the gun out, wrapped in a handkerchief. "Why do you want it?"

"I want to know how many cartridges have been fired. Look, you break it there." I snatched it out of his hands. There would presumably have been six bullets in the gun originally, now there were only four. And I didn't think more than one had been used to silence

Annette. Mark took the gun away and carefully cleaned it with his handkerchief before he threw it back approximately where we'd found it. "What now?" he asked.

"We have to find the other bullet, of course." I had hideous visions of Philip's discovering how he'd been mocked, made use of, love desecrated, firing point-blank at her and turning the second bullet on himself. Only in that case, where was Philip? You can't commit suicide with a gun and just vanish off the scene.

"Did we look everywhere?" I asked. It was a big room, I hadn't looked further than Annette's body. Mark, too, looked almost at the end of his tether, but he went back to the room. He came out to say there was nothing, nothing. We ought to get the police, he added. There must be a telephone.

I could imagine it, a pale yellow affair beside a fluffy bed. The next instant I was on my feet and stumbling on the stairs.

"Where now?" Mark said, but I didn't answer him. I'd caught sight of something winking on the dark step. I picked it up and stood looking at it in the palm of my hand. It was a little silver fish, the scales made flexible so that it trembles in your hand. There was a hook in the fish's mouth and attached to that a little bit of chain and on the chain a key.

"What on earth's that?"

"A key ring," I told him. "And the last time I saw it, it was in my son's hand. That's the key of his bicycle. You have to padlock them. Now we know he was down here. And we've been forgetting X all this time. Of course he and Annette were in it together." I was hauling myself up by the banisters as I spoke; each step seemed a mile high. "They lured Philip here because he was a danger to them, and afterwards he'd be bound to realize she was a danger, too. Come to that, she'd

179

probably been a danger all along." I reached the first landing and automatically started unlocking doors. My subconsciousness registered that Annette's room was just what I'd anticipated, except that the telephone was two pale shades of gray. Her coat lay across the bed. For some reason that seemed to set the seal on her death. "She could have had something on him, he'd be the only person who could identify her with Philip's disappearance, probably he thought he couldn't afford to let her go on living."

It's strange how near you can come to the truth without actually falling over it.

Mark had followed me to the doorway. "Someone was in a hurry," he said, and I noticed for the first time that the room was in a state of complete chaos. There was a writing desk against one wall, whose drawers had been torn out and contents spilled; the bed was rumpled, even the lingerie drawers gaped open. Not that I cared who had been looking for what, I was a near-maniac looking for my son—living or dead—my son.

"The attic!" I whispered. I wouldn't say good-bye to hope, there was still a chance, someone had broken that window. Up I went, and the stairs rose one by one in front of me and defied me to reach the next tread. I ignored other closed doors. At the end of the last stairway the key stood in the attic door. It turned so smooth, so smooth, someone must have just oiled it. I put on the light. The place had been used as a box-room, though it was intended for servants' quarters, there was even a little washbasin in a corner. It's odd how rich people so often can't bring themselves to part with trash. That room was full of flotsam and jetsam, out-of-date chairs, a roll of carpet, baggage, a cupboard, boxes of papers, a second roll of carpet under the window. Only when I got closer I saw it wasn't carpet after all, but my son, Philip.

I was down on my knees in a flash. The clever lad, I was saying in my heart, the clever lad. Breaking the window to get air. Because it was a small room with a low ceiling and the door fitted tight. He must have broken the pane with his clenched fists, because his hands were tied together, and there was blood on them. Perhaps he hadn't thought about oxygen, after all, perhaps he'd hoped to attract attention, though he must have known there wasn't a chance in a hundred, this isolated place, no houses near, only the dreary garden and the common land beyond. But, again, he was like his father, he'd expect a helicopter or a raven to come by at the crucial moment and raise the alarm. His last emotion must have been one of intense surprise that his luck should have deserted him at last.

He'd been knocked out; there was considerable discoloration over one brow, and he wasn't conscious, but he hadn't been much disfigured. All the same, I thought Miss Snake Muir would think twice before she referred to him as your handsome son. Mark came stumbling through the debris and stooped down beside me.

"Is he . . .?" breathing, he meant. I was feeling furiously for a pulse. I couldn't find it, but I reminded myself that meant nothing, I've never been good at finding pulses.

Mark's hand opened his shirt, he stooped, putting his ear to Philip's chest. "He has a chance," he said. "Keep him warm. I'll fetch a doctor. Quicker than ringing up."

"What are you waiting for?" I screamed, pulling off my coat and wrapping it around my son. "And if he's at a deathbed drag him away." I didn't care about anyone's deathbed that night but Philip's. "How about the police?" I added as the door swung open.

"Them, too."

As the door closed I forgot Mark's existence. I had Philip in my arms, he seemed awfully cold. He was such a responsive child, even as a baby; I'd never seen him like this. Obstinate, difficult, antagonistic even, but never untouched, shut away behind a barrier I couldn't pierce. I bowed myself over him, giving him the kiss of life, as we'd been taught at the Town Hall lectures. I couldn't believe that I, who had given him the priceless gift at the beginning, couldn't renew it now. What else are mothers for? I thought. Not to adjudicate, not to command or to make claims, to give life and go on giving it, and know that that's the greatest privilege accorded to the human creature. Poor Miss Muir, poor spinsters, poor all childless women—making love, being secure, what did any of that matter compared with this priceless gift?

Suddenly, with no warning, the light went out. A faulty bulb, I thought, or wiring disturbed by the storm. It seemed the ultimate *comble,* a kind of warning of the darkness to come. "It won't be for long," I whispered to Philip, who was in the dark anyway, so would notice no change. "Mark will be back."

It's strange how darkness seems to change the world. Darkness without, darkness within. I was surprised to realize that the worst of the storm was already over; the rain was still coming down in buckets, steady and straight, lashing the world, but the thunder was a soft roll and the lightning had stopped. I missed the noise, I even wished the jay would come back. The room darkened, and it was difficult to see the time by my absurd little watch. I began to curse Mark for being so long. Surely there'd be doctors—anyway, why hadn't the police come? I strained my ears in case they had arrived and were absorbed in Annette. Not that that made sense. I thought, I'll ring them again. Perhaps Mark's still looking for a doctor, didn't wait to telephone, doesn't know where the station is. It's at moments like these that all the intolerable contingencies spring to mind, a car overturned, Mark having an embolism—not that he looked the type—a road accident . . .

"I shall be back in a moment," I whispered to my son. He was still breathing, but it didn't seem to me that it was getting any stronger. Up here the cold seemed intense. I pulled up the roll of carpet to support his head and started to make my way to the door. The low ceiling added to the room's darkness. I banged into something and almost fell, but pulled myself up and reached the door. The handle seemed stiff, or the damp had swollen the wood. I tugged, but it didn't open. I addressed it in terms that would have made Mr. Crook turn puce. Still it didn't move. It must have been a full minute before I realized it didn't open because it was locked—on the other side.

Even so, it was another minute before the full implications of that came home. At first I thought, The clot! Who does he suppose is going to break in and attack us here? Any normal person passing would suppose the house was empty. Unless they went around to the back, of course, and why on earth should they do that? When the obvious explanation did get through I still didn't believe it, not just because it was too bad a thing to happen to me, but because it was too bad to happen to anyone. I had to spell the words out. Philip and I are alone here in a locked room, in a closed house. No one knows where we are. Mark is not coming back with a doctor. Mark is not coming back. Period. And nobody knew I was here.

I could hear myself gaily telling Miss Muir I was going to the Burgoyne. When I didn't come back that night she might think it odd, but she wouldn't take any steps. A night on the tiles, she might think, not what would have been acceptable in her day, but we have to move with the times. When I didn't come back at all but the milk and papers continued to be delivered, she might get suspicious and go to the police. And then I remembered she was probably in the plot, too. There was no one anywhere . . . Even Annette couldn't be questioned, her disappearance wouldn't surprise anyone particularly, and in any case until the murder inquiry opened she was a free agent. As for Philip—oh, he might have run away to sea or something. Even if anyone did examine Boxwood it would be too late, a great deal too late.

There was still Crook, but I hadn't taken Crook into my confidence, and he'd warned me he couldn't make bricks unless he was given the right amount of straw. I stumbled back to the window and pushed it up. The rain pounded down. I yelled, and my voice came slamming contemptuously back at me. To my own ears it didn't sound human. Those bloody jays! someone would say comfortably. If this was a film, there would be a tree growing conveniently near the window, a walnut tree for choice. I would scramble out, down the partisan branches, get help, save my son. That 'ud be a turn-up for the book. They'd probably give me a medal— Mother of the Year. Only there wasn't a tree; there wasn't even a drainpipe. There were no bedclothes to knot together, and if I jumped, it would be a case of bodies to right of them, bodies to left of them. Reason and good sense were gone now, with the light and hope.

I lifted my voice and called to my unknown God. "They say You're good at working miracles," I challenged Him, "work one now for me."

I suppose God gets used to this sort of insolence. Anyway, He didn't appear to take any notice.

When the light came on suddenly, I didn't believe it. A minute later feet sounded on the stairs. Perhaps I'd misjudged Mark, after all. Only these were solid clumping feet, policemen's feet. They came as far as the landing, a hand turned the doorknob.

"It's locked," I shouted. "We're both locked in."

A voice screamed over the banister. "Both up here," it said. "Do your stuff." I rushed across and thumped on the door.

"That's no good," said the voice. I thought it must be Crook, who gives you the impression he can work miracles without bothering the Almighty, only it didn't sound like him. A key rattled, the door began to open.

"Old trick," said the voice. "One key in the servants' quarters opens the lot. Opens possibilities, too."

I fell back, feeling like the mother whale defending her wounded calf. There she stood in the doorway, beaming, rosy as a vampire, gloating over me and my son.

"Keep back!" I commanded. At least, I thought that's what I said, but she pushed me out of the way as though I were made of straw. Down she went on her plump knees; she turned my son's face to the light.

"Where's the fire?" she asked comfortably. "He's going to be all right." She opened a huge white plastic bag and brought out a little bottle. "Brandy," she confided. "Never go anywhere without it. Come to that, you look as though you need it more than he does."

I found my voice. "He's been there since Friday."

"Had a cousin, Barty his name was—ship torpedoed by the Germans—stuck it out on a raft eight days. Right as rain now, married with five children. They're a tough lot, the present young, have to be, bombs, rumors, all that caper."

She had unscrewed the flask and was trying to tilt a little brandy into Philip's mouth.

185

"No," I said. "No."

She looked up at me. "What's the matter? It's not poisoned. Prove it." She put the cup to her lips and drained it. "Concussion," she announced. "Must have fallen and hit his head."

The jay must have come back and perched on the window sill. It was screaming in my ear.

"Concussion!" I said. "He's been attacked. Did you notice his hands?"

"Glass from the window. Not serious, though. If he'd been out when they put him here he couldn't have done that, could he?" She whisked a handkerchief not much smaller than a sheet out of her capacious pocket. "Any water in that tap? Damp this, dear. Not much else we can do really, till the doctor comes."

"I'm surprised you haven't brought him in your pocket," I said.

"And Mr. Crook," she went on. "He'll be here any minute, I shouldn't wonder. It's an ill wind that blows no one any good. There's a man I've always wanted to meet."

"I don't understand," I told her, with the screaming patience of someone feeling in the dark. "I didn't telephone him . . ."

"That was me. They didn't leave much to chance, did they? Phone disconnected, light turned off at the main . . ."

"That would be Mark when he left," I interrupted. In a way that seemed to me the worst thing he had done, deliberately to engulf us in the unpitying dark. "What made you suppose this was a job for Mr. Crook?"

She smiled at me, rueful, apologetic, but accusing, too. "You must think me a fool—that story about going to the Burgoyne in flat heels and a head scarf. Probably wouldn't get as far as the snack bar. So I telephoned, and of course they didn't know anything. I tried both names. I'd realized who he was by then—that's when I began to Get the Wind Up. I mean, you going out into an unspecified destination with a criminal—it always sounds so much more exciting on the television than in real life." She squeezed out her handkerchief and sponged Philip's face. "I watched the car," she continued, "it went west, not Up West. You're not going to any bang-up restaurant, I told myself, so I thought, Call Mr. Crook. So fortunate you happened to mention his name. He wasn't there, but his partner said he'd locate him."

"Why did you tell him Virginia Water?"

"I couldn't think of anywhere else. I knew you'd been there the day before, you did look so guilty, and then I put my thinking cap on, and I remembered Samson had a house there and there was a picture in the paper of Mrs. Samson in the garden—such an ugly house—and he'd been arrested for her husband's murder—ah, that sounds like someone arriving. Doctor, I hope. Sent my companion for him," she added explanatorily. "The one who appeared on my doorstep like an answer to a prayer, asking for you. Something about a cable . . ."

"Did he happen to mention who he was?" It occurred to me we might all be dead and in a world where nothing functions the way you'd expect.

"Said he was Philip's father, and from the likeness between them I'd say it was most probably true." She looked up, a veritable daughter of the sun. "You'd better take my place," she said. "He's opening his eyes, and he won't want to find himself in the arms of a strange woman."

I didn't have that opportunity, though, because the doctor came in and swept us all aside.

"Let's have some air," said an autocratic voice. "Well, he doesn't believe in doing things by halves, does he? What happened? Or wouldn't you know?" And that, if you please, wasn't to me, the boy's mother, but to Miss Sixty-Plus-and-Never-Been-Kissed.

I was like someone caught up in a whirlwind. I'd always believed that in a crisis I'd keep my head, foil the bank robbers, trick the villains, and all I'd been able to do was bring my worst enemy to the danger spot and let myself be bamboozled like a child. And all the while old bumbling Angela Muir had shown herself to be worth ten of me. Ten? Twenty? A hundred.

"A hundred," I repeated impressively.

"You'd better have that brandy now," said Angela.

"I thought you were in it," I told her. I had the feeling I ought to give her something, and all I had to give her was the truth.

"Go ahead and cry if you want to," the old thing said. "It's often a release. All this nonsense they teach you about the stiff upper lip, best way of getting paralyzed I know." I sensed vaguely she was rattling on to give me an opportunity to pull myself together. "I know it's usual to think of spinsters as a kind of aging dinosaur, but it never seems to occur to people we must have had something to survive at all. Goodness knows everything's against us. We have to fight for ourselves every inch of the way, we get called Auntie by perfect strangers, and there isn't even anyone to bring us a cup of tea in bed. Do you realize, my dear, there was actually a time in the Middle Ages when unmarried women were conscripted as domestic slaves to the married? And really, points of view haven't changed much. We'll get old Aunt Annie to babysit, open the house, walk the dog, look after the children when Mum's down with flu or fancies a weekend away, *she'd* be no temptation to the most lecherous husband. I was at a convent school," she ran on happily. "It's wonderful what you pick up there, we were told that in heaven we shall walk in front of the wives, because we've been denied so much earthly bliss."

"All husbands aren't angels," I heard myself interrupt.

"Lovely though to have someone always on the premises to Scrap With. That's one of the things one misses so if one isn't married. And there's no substitute. No sense having a dog because they're so affectionate they never scrap, and cats are far too superior to come down to your level. Ah, here they come."

Men poured into the room, or so it seemed; a number had arrived unnoticed or else I was seeing double. Two men in uniform barged past carrying a chair. They packed Philip in.

"Straight to the hospital," said the doctor.

"Is the mother here? Oh? Are you coming with us?" one of the men asked.

"Of course I'm coming," I said. I put my foot firmly on the floor to make certain it was really where I thought it was, it had a distressing tendency to move like a wave. It had risen a bit higher than I anticipated. The sound of my foot on the bare boards was like a hare stamping. Someone laughed gently. It reminded me of George. I said as much. "George!" I said.

"I wondered when you were going to recognize me," said my ex-husband, amiable as always. I knew then that I was crazy, because how could George be in New Zealand and in this room?

"I'm delirious," I told everyone seriously. "My husband" (it's funny how I still thought of him as my husband) "is in New Zealand. Delirious. But not drunk," I added. "I didn't take the whiskey, not even a drop. Listen, I can say delirious perfectly distinctly." I said it again for good measure. "That's funny, isn't it? Deliriously funny."

"I'd better give her a shot, too," suggested an impersonal voice.

"No," I shouted, "not me. There's been too much shooting already. Did you find her?"

"Are you coming in the ambulance, madam?"

More people seemed to be coming into the room all the time. "Not now," I heard the doctor say. "This boy's going straight to hospital. And the mother isn't fit to be questioned; I'll sign a certificate if need be. If you want a story you'd better ask Mr. Crook, and if you can make any sense out of that you'll be lucky."

It was the first time that I realized Mr. Crook was in the room. I don't know how long he'd been there. You wouldn't have thought anyone so blustering could make himself appear so invisible.

"Come on, Bert," said one of the men with the chair. "The mother's not coming."

"Of course she's not coming," cried Miss Muir exuberantly. "No sense till the boy can talk to her. But it's all right, I'll hold the fort till then, I'll come with you. Well, what else are aunties for?"

"I think," said George deprecatingly (if it was George), "she's going to pass out."

"I do like a little co-operation in a client," said Crook enthusiastically. "Even a rozzer can't hope to get a story out of a lady in a coma."

And that's the last thing I remember.

XII

Considering we hadn't met for nearly seven years it was odd how normal it seemed to open my eyes and find George standing beside me with a tray in his hands.

"Make yourself at home!" I said generously. It took me a minute to realize what had happened. "Philip!" I exclaimed, starting to get up.

He pushed me back. "He's going to be all right. Concussion, probably due to a fall after they put him in the attic."

"He must have come round by now," I said.

"Give him time. It's nature's way. So long as he's out he's safe from the press and the police—and you," he added coolly. "And nothing's going to happen to him, he's being guarded like the Grand Cham Diamond. Police watch all round the clock. No one's going in till the doctor gives the word."

"If the doctor imagines that prohibition applies to me, he must be mad," I said. "I'm going round at once."

"He's in Windsor," said George.

I stopped. Well, naturally, they'd take him to the nearest hospital, I should have thought of that. "I don't

191

know what you're doing here," I told him. "I thought you were in New Zealand."

"So I was," George agreed. "But though you can divorce a husband from his wife, you can't divorce a father from his son, and though, my darling, my admiration for you is unbounded, there are occasions when a male parent has his points. So when Bill cabled . . ."

"Bill?"

"Bill Shrubsall. You remember him surely, the one you thought too frivolous to be a godfather . . ."

"Of course I remember him," I said. "I just didn't understand where he came in."

"He's been keeping me in touch all this time. The minute this thing broke he sent his cable and I came back on the first available plane. I came to the flat to be met on the doorstep by a veritable lioness."

"A man-eater," I agreed. "It's a wonder you escaped with your full complement of limbs."

"She hailed me as an answer to a prayer. You must be Philip's father, she said."

"Did Bill send her a cable, too?"

"There is a likeness," submitted George. "Well, she was sure you'd be at Virginia Water . . ."

"Did she explain why?"

"You don't ask lionesses for explanations, you just go along with them. She got this hired car from a local garage, she'd have called down a chariot of fire from heaven, if need be. I wish I'd known you'd got her for a neighbor. It would have save me a lot of anxiety."

I nearly fainted for the second time. "You shouldn't have worried," I said politely. "Incidentally, how does your wife feel about you crossing the world at a minute's notice?"

"You tell me," said George.

"You don't mean to say you haven't married again?" George put back his head and let out a bellow of laughter that wouldn't have shamed Miss Muir. "Once bitten, twice shy. Mind you, I never saw Bill's handwriting on an envelope without anticipating wedding bells on this side of the ocean."

"If you're divorced you get married in a registrar's," I pointed out, "and there are no wedding bells there."

"You haven't changed a bit," said George. "It's a funny thing, this is about the first time I've been able to do something for you. In the old days it was always you being the bear-leader—practically the first time the bear's managed to edge into the picture."

The telephone rang and he went to answer it. "No comment," I heard him say. He crossed to the window and looked out. Then he threw up the sash. "I'll give you a couple of minutes to clear the street," he called down. "Then I'll douse you with a bucket of slops if I have to go round to the pig market to collect them. Press," he added to me, slamming the window down.

"Anyone could tell you'd been in the outbacks," I gasped. "You can't talk to people like that in a free Britain."

"You'll have to educate me, won't you?" said George. "Oh come, you know we were made for each other. By the way, we have an appointment with Crook at twelve, if you're up to it. And the hospital says you can ring up at eleven for the latest report."

Waiting till I could get through I let myself recall the events of last night. They were still a bit hazy, but they were becoming clearer. Much later in the evening, in London with Crook and George in attendance, I'd talked to the police. Both had insisted on being present and Mall had more or less gracefully given way. I had an opportunity of realizing the wisdom of those who won't talk to authority until they've got a legal beagle at their elbow. At every turn Crook sidestepped them. "What's the use of asking my client what she thought?"

he'd demand in truculent tones. "She's not here to speculate, just to give you the facts as she sees them." Operative words being the last four. A lot of things came out, of course, that I'd tried to suppress—the authorship of the letters, Philip's flight—you couldn't call it anything else—from Oxton, my first visit to Virginia Water. This time Mall didn't doodle at all. At the end he remarked sourly that I might have saved the police a lot of trouble if I'd come clean at the start.

"That's the worst of taxpayers," said Crook sunnily, "they do like to get value for money."

When I'd signed my statement, and this time I didn't knowingly conceal a thing, George took me home. I didn't remember much after that.

"Did I have a sleeping pill?" I called out.

"Two," said George.

"One's the normal dose," I told him.

George appeared in the doorway with a tea towel tied round his waist. "But you're an abnormal woman, darling."

At eleven o'clock, as agreed, I rang the hospital. The news was quite hopeful, we might even be able to see Philip that afternoon for about five seconds. Doctor was very pleased with his progress. I got dressed and looked out of the window. The photographers were still there.

"You'd think they'd have enough pictures of me to fill an album," I said.

"Can't have too much of a good thing," beamed George, bumbling around the flat under the impression that he was making it spick and span. It went through my mind that perhaps he was now their main target. It's the kind of story the public laps up—husband returning from the other side of the world in the Nick of Time . . .

"But you're not my husband any more," I said.

"You can't strike out fourteen years with the stroke of a pen."

"The law says you can."

"The law, as is well known, is a hass. And if you don't agree, why aren't you Mrs. Somebody Else by now? Don't tell me you haven't had plenty of chances."

He rang up the local car-rental office and said he'd like the chauffeur who'd taken a couple to Virginia Water yesterday afternoon. "Lady fixed it, I think," he said. "She didn't happen to mention it to me," he explained, hanging up the receiver, "but it was a pretty safe bet. By the way, she's coming along with us."

"Angela Muir?"

"Someone was inspired when they christened her."

I gaped. I felt as if I were in a Looking Glass world where everything goes the wrong way.

When we went down she was waiting in the hall, dressed to kill, swinging amber chain, gold link bracelet, hat decorated with a couple of pineapples and a bunch of cherries.

"I'll go first," she offered. "Then I can Bear the Brunt."

She opened the front door and all the cameras swung into position. I had to admit she was worth a plate in that getup, with the story attached. She hauled out another of her huge handkerchiefs and waved it in a grand gesture. A sudden burst of choking and coughing ensued, in the course of which George seized my arm, pulled my scarf over my mouth and rushed me down the steps into the car. By the time the ghouls had recovered, the driver had pressed the starter and we were off.

"Snuff," explained a beaming Miss Muir. "Never known it to fail."

"You can probably get six months for that," I warned her.

"Not to worry," said George. "They won't want to make themselves look sillier than they are. I've known chaps who could stand up to a firing squad who wilted at the first sign of ridicule."

"I suppose in Fiji or wherever this sort of thing happens all the time."

"How I'd love to go there," sighed the romantic Angela from the back seat. "Of course, you can travel in your mind, but that's a circumscribed area."

You can say that again, I thought.

"You'd like it, Meg," George encouraged me. He only called me Meg when he wanted to wheedle me into doing something I didn't want to do. "Lovely sun, bathing, freedom . . ." He lifted an arm and described a semicircle.

"Lovely to be young," sighed Miss Muir. "Future ahead, new life—anyone can molder when they're old like me."

"You'll never be old," said George affectionately. "Die a hundred years young, I wouldn't wonder."

It was a relief, really, when this mutual admiration came to an end and we reached Crook's office. He was sitting behind the desk, which was every whit as cluttered as before, looking as fresh as a new-minted half-crown, only, naturally, much heavier. He welcomed us all, asked about Philip (characteristically he'd rung the hospital himself), congratulated Miss Muir on her hat and said, "Now we'll fit in the last bits of the jigsaw. Always a satisfaction to see the pattern complete. You'll remember, sugar, I told you that when we knew why Samson didn't try to defend himself we'd be halfway to the solution?"

"And now you know?" I suggested.

Crook was nothing if not generous. "You put the key right in my hand and I never saw you do it," he acknowledged handsomely. "Y'see, it's a situation I know pretty well, sitting behind the desk, waiting for the un-known. A lot of chaps prefer to call after dark—well, they have their reasons, and you can't always be dead sure what those reasons are going to be."

"But you don't carry a gun," I protested.

"I don't need one, not so long as I have Bill. Better than a brigade of Household Cavalry, and my visitors know it. Even in my grave I'd be sorry for anyone with Bill on his tail. Well, Samson not having a Bill, he has to rely on mechanical aid. One reason why he puts a lot of space between him and the incoming client. Give him plenty of time to snatch the gun from the drawer and go into action."

"But he didn't," I protested.

"He didn't because someone stopped him. Figure it out for yourself, sugar. Bell rings, door opens, he's behind the desk, and Murder comes in. He'd know, you always know. Down goes his hand for the hot rod that's cooler than a soda fountain. Only—it ain't avail-able."

"It was in the drawer," I assured him. "I saw it."

"Sure it was in the drawer. So was the key."

"That's right. I knocked it out of the lock when I touched it."

"I'd say that was a case of history repeating itself. You see, if you adjust these keys right you can fix it that the lightest touch will dislodge them. He tugs at the drawer—hey, presto! it's locked. Before he can stoop and retrieve the key, Murder's on him, he doesn't stand an earthly. Simple when you know how—and realize this was a two-man stunt— Well, one man, one woman."

"Annette?" I exclaimed.

"I don't see who else it could be. No one else has the come-and-go in that office. She helps to set the stage, told you that much herself, writes the letters, gets out the envelopes, I wouldn't be surprised. She knows who's coming—mind you, I don't say she had it in specially for you, you just happened to fit the pattern. Off she goes, has her alibi nice and pat, enter second murderer."

"And that was Mark?" I was beginning to feel giddy.

"Never does to take anything for granted," said Crook seriously. "*He* says he had an appointment for eight-thirty. *We* know there must have been someone there before eight, when you come onto the scene. You know how the police realized he was expected that night? Payment, cash or kind, was made to their overlord at regular intervals, once a month, once a quarter, so it was easy for them to make a short list, from the index, you understand, of anyone who could have been there that night. But the cards didn't give a specific time. And who says Spurr was expected at eight-thirty?"

"Spurr himself."

"Pre-cisely." Crook beamed.

Miss Muir looked as if she'd had a vision from on high.

"He comes in seven-thirty, as arranged—this is my story, agreed, but I'll bet a month's pay the facts corroborate it—comes head down for Samson, knowing the chap won't have time to produce the gun."

"Wouldn't he check?" I interrupted. "Samson, I mean?"

"You know how they say the husband is always the last to know. Samson knew the kind of woman he'd married, but he believed she realized which side her bread was buttered. I doubt if it ever went through his mind that she might renege on him. *Envelopes, gun, the lot? Anything before I go?* Probably went like a bomb, week after week. I'd say a hammer, one of those with heavy heads and long handles, was as likely a weapon as any. You can do a lot of damage with a hammer. There was a case I had in the war not unlike this one. Used a hammer there. Have it in a briefcase, whirl it out from under your arm—plenty of places to hide a hammer, all the building and repair work that's going on. Lot of chaps if they find a serviceable hammer that wasn't there last night aren't going to report it. I doubt if we ever trace that, not unless Spurr sings. And he could, you know, like a blooming canary bird. Well, with his partner on the mortuary slab, there's no one to sing against him, he's got the field to himself. He gets out, probably wearing a plastic mac or something, waits for you, nips off while you're still recovering from shock— and that's where he has to play it cool. He has to find out what you're going to do. So he waits till you give him the sayso."

"I never saw him," I protested.

"Now, sugar, that's not what you told the police. Nor me, come to that. Loud and clear, you said, 'There he was . . .' "

"The man getting the cigarettes?" I shouted.

"Who else? Y'see, you've got two choices. Either you ring the police right away, and he'll get that message quick enough when the cars come rolling in, or you'll take your evidence—and remember he's in Annette's confidence, he knows what the evidence is—and oil out. And being a woman of sense you'll make sure there's no one to watch you do the oiling. So he waits to see the window curtain shift. That's his cue. Into the box he goes, dials Samson's number."

"I mightn't have answered," I objected.

"Some risks you have to take. And there's something about a ringing phone . . ."

"I'd come out of the grave to answer my phone if it rang," said Miss Muir simply.

"By the time you're in the street he's out of sight. Your next movements don't interest him. He's established a kind of alibi, very fact that the phone was answered would make people believe Samson was alive at the time, goes along to a bar where he's known . . ."

"If he had an alibi, why did the police pick him up at all?"

"Because they only had his word for it that his date was eight-thirty. Could have been eight. They didn't know about you then, remember."

"It's all very complicated," I murmured.

"It's like a ball of string," said Miss Muir. "Get the right end and you never a tangle. If not . . ." She shrugged and one of the dangling cherries bounced off her ear. It was a large serviceable ear, well attuned for listening.

"What Spurr didn't allow for was you taking the envelope. That upsets all his schemes, and the other thing he hadn't allowed for was Annette's substituting one envelope for another."

"*Annette* did that?"

"Oh, I think so. Who else? Mind you, I don't know what her original idea was, and now we're never likely to know for sure, but I think her and her husband were in this racket together; she got a lot of the ammunition and Samson levied the tax. Nothing new about that. Similar teams have been operating since the beginning of time. Maybe he suspected her of double-crossing him, maybe he even did think of divorce, though I'm not sure he'd have dared bring a charge, most likely it seemed to her it would be nice to be a rich widow. Or she may have had a real yen for Spurr. He was one of the victims all right; he wouldn't mind hanging up his hat on a golden hook behind the wife's door. Only Samson mustn't suspect. So she makes a lot of play with your lad's letters—oh yes, he never cottoned onto that, on his own why should be, a lot of buff envelopes with different postmarks. . . ?"

"But why Philip?" My blood was clamoring. I thought

it was a good thing someone had shot Annette, it put temptation out of my path.

"Rich Da in the Lakes—and even little fish are sweet. Not likely to rumble her, he was over the moon, you said. That's another thing, you know." His voice took on a graver note. "He's going to be suffering from shock when he comes round, and not just because of that bang on the head. Not nice to find your first true ladylove has been milking you from the word Go. Still, he'll not let them wreck him, he's your son, ain't he? Only these things take a little time. I'd say the photo —if there ever was a photo—and the check were all part of the plot. Like the lady lapwing that don't mind who she involves so long as she leads you away from *her* nest. She'd need patience, they'd both need that, but at last it's the time, the place and the loved one all together. And you do just what she'd expect. She must have thought she had it made."

"You mean, I didn't call the police?"

"That's what I mean."

"And you think Annette was really in love with Mark Spurr all the time?"

I felt like someone going down a very steep hill. I had to put down my foot with great care each time, no sense trying to run. Crook, on the other hand, seemed to be skimming along like some gigantic chamois.

"I think the only person Annette really loved was Annette. As for your lad, well, face it, sugar, he was a pigeon designed to throw dust in her husband's eyes."

"Pigeons don't throw dust," I objected.

"Don't give me that, sugar, you know what I mean. Well, that's Samson out of the way. Only something happens they hadn't allowed for. You go into your Florence Nightingale act and think you'll save another victim. So—Spurr gets pulled in. And then you play your second trump. It was me," he added modestly, "who suggested to the police it might be a good idea to let Spurr out on a short lead. They could gather him in again if they wanted to, he hadn't been tried for any crime. And it was just possible he might lead us to the haven where he would be."

"And he did?" I still felt light-headed.

"With your invaluable help. When you're going in your mourning weeds, just remember you saved your boy's life. That's something any mum might be proud of."

"I wouldn't give two straws for any mother who didn't," I cried furiously. "What I don't understand is why they pulled Philip back again."

"Not them, sugar. You. Pulling him in, I mean. Their plan was that you should carry the can. And you go and upset things for them, first by pulling Spurr in, and then getting him out again."

"Why didn't they like that?" I demanded.

"Because the police are like a pack of hounds. If one fox goes to earth, they ain't satisfied till they've broken up another. And the obvious person to put in Spurr's place is you. And if that happens your boy, Philip, is going to have his hat in the ring before you can say Knife. And being your son, he won't do things by halves. He'll pour it all out like those ancients emptying their cornucopia at the foot of the goddess—letters, check, the lot. You can't suppose Annette's going to like that. Someone's going to suggest right away that Samson's makin' a beeline for the divorce courts, and bein' a rich widow's one thing and a divorced wife with no claims to alimony's different again. It's not as though he had much of this world's goods, from all accounts. No, I think they'd take a lot of chances to stop your lad's mouth. Well, we know they did."

"You all know so much more about it than I do," I said.

"You know he got this phone call and told his mate he was coming to London to see you. You know that ain't so. You know there's only one person he'd come down for, bar yourself, and that's sweet little Annette. That was the beginning of it all. I'd say he was met at the railway station by Spurr—he don't have to recognize him, but anyway Spurr wouldn't have to lean very heavily on the make-up box to look as different as can be: Charlie Chaplin mustache, library horners, black out a tooth, perhaps. Trouble with criminals is they're yellow, they want to be a hundred per cent safe. And it can't be done. They'd have served themselves by waiting a bit, seeing which way the police cat was going to jump, but no, they don't have the nerve, so it was to be *out* for Philip Ross."

"They must have been mad," I said scornfully. "If I wouldn't sit on the touchline when Philip was threatened, what did they think I was going to do when he disappeared?"

"According to their plan, that was covered. Officially he'd come to see you. That might be a tale, but it didn't prove he came down to see Annette. Might have found he couldn't stand the strain, inquiries, publicity, probably the push from college when the truth came out, story of the check circulating—they couldn't have made that stick, seeing the check was destroyed and Samson not there to give evidence, but most people don't worry about what happened, only about how it looks. No, it wouldn't seem unreasonable if he'd made a bolt for it —that's their argument. There's a slight danger, of course, someone could see him and Spurr meeting at London, but you know what these big stations are, you can have a birth, a death, and half the people present won't notice. And even Annette and Spurr must have recognized you can't sew everything up so tight no stitch will ever slip. Down they come, here's

Annette—'Darling, how sweet of you, I'm in such trouble, I've no one else to turn to . . .' " He was enjoying himself like crazy.

I thought of something else. "Why did she have to bring Spurr into it, at this stage, I mean? Philip isn't a baby, he can travel under his own steam."

"They don't want him asking around for Boxwood, maybe hiring a car—he didn't have his own, remember . . . No, this was their best bet. They have a nice cup of coffee . . ."

"Did he bring the gun?" I interrupted.

"Oh, I think she had that, don't you? I think if Spurr had seen the gun he'd have got it immobilized somehow. When thieves get together it's always unsafe when one has a lethal weapon and the other's unarmed. So, like I said, they pour him a cup of coffee—we know that must be right, because the tray was found in the kitchen later, with three cups, none of them empty, and one of them handsomely laced with dope. Tell me, sugar, did your son take it—sugar, I mean?"

"No," I said. "Neither of us did—do," I amended quickly.

"Maybe Annette didn't know that, or more likely she did know, but took a chance that he'd be the perfect little gent, drinking whatever's put in front of him. They'd have to add some sweetener to the cup to deaden the bitter taste of the drug. Only it would explain why he only just sipped at the stuff instead of swallowing it down and letting them get on with the job."

"Which was?"

"Well, sugar, ain't it obvious? They can't afford to let him get back into circulation, they don't want to chance another murder charge, but if he's dumped somewhere not too easy to find, but where he could have slipped or decided to make an end of things— Now, no sense looking so green, I always warned you it was a dangerous job getting born, and if you didn't like it you should have stayed put. Anyway, I'll tell you one thing I'm pretty sure they didn't intend and that was that anybody—anybody—should find him in an attic in Annette's house. Only they made one big mistake. Oh, they made others, but this is the kind you never get forgiven."

"I'm sure you're going to tell us what it is," I said. I felt George's hand press closely on mine, but to hell with tact, I thought. What does this man think he is? A stage manager?

"They forgot the fifth ace—they thought if they held four the game had to be theirs. But fate, who don't know anything about fair play, keeps the fifth up her sleeve, and that's the winning ace of all, and this time she decided to play it on the side of virtue."

"You make it sound better than Sherlock Holmes," breathed that fool Angela Muir, whose eyes had widened till you could practically have set teacups in them.

"You could call the story Saved by the Bell," Crook beamed. "Because that's actually what it was. There they were with everything set when—enter the fifth ace, name of Maxwell Price. Well, you remember him, sugar. It was you found his card in the hall."

I was feeling utterly bewildered again. "You mean, *he* was in it, too?"

"Not their plot—fate's. Price has been interviewed, says he was staying at Windsor and heard there was a house not far from Virginia Water coming into the market any day now, thought it might be just what he and his wife were looking for, so came over without an appointment, took his chance, see? Naturally, when Annette and Spurr hear the bell they start to wonder if the jig's up. I mean, who's likely to come calling at a house at the end of nowhere, unless it's the boys in blue?"

"I suppose they could refuse to open the door."

"With the house open, and anyway, the boy's there. He's going to think it rum, ain't he? Mind you, he's supposed to be out for the count by this time, but he ain't co-operating. There he is, sitting as bright as a button, twirling his coffee cup, might even have offered to answer the door. Wouldn't surprise me at all, because that 'ud give Spurr a chance to come up behind him and deal the knockout blow. Just to knock the sense out of him, mark you. When he's found in one of those gravel pits in all that wasteland behind the house or wherever his ultimate destination was to be—there's a pond there that's going to surprise a lot of people on the last day when the waters yield up the dead that are in them—a court's going to return an open verdict. Down he goes like a log, Spurr collects him like a sack of potatoes and up the stairs they go. Safest place really. If you like a house and one of the attics is locked and the owner explains the key is missing, they can get another made, only junk there anyway . . ."

"That's when the key ring fell out of his pocket," I said.

"All unbeknownst to Spurr. No sense blaming him, though. You missed it yourself first go-off."

"Why tie his hands if he was unconscious?" I demanded.

I heard George sigh. I knew it meant What does that matter now? but to me everything mattered, even the smallest detail.

"If you've ever tried carrying an unconscious body you'd be surprised what arms can do—they jerk around, wrap themselves round your neck . . ."

"I had a dog once," contributed Miss Muir brightly, "took it to the vet, brought it back, still very dopey, no control at all, legs all over the place, knocked my hat off, might have been an octopus."

I wondered if there was any question to which she didn't know the answer.

"Annette meantime rushes the tray into the kitchen, opens the door. No policeman, just a chap with a visiting card. I bet she could have crowned him. Still, she lets him in, might look rum if she didn't. New-made widows shouldn't be entertaining folk they don't like a stranger to see, and gossip gets around in the country the same as it does anywhere else. This Price seems to have been a noticing sort of chap, says he didn't go above the ground floor, realized it wasn't just what they wanted, bit on the big side, but he did see the kitchen. I bet Mrs. P. put him up to that, seeing the amount of time ladies spend there nowadays, and he did remember seeing a tray with three nearly full coffee cups on it. Says he hopes he didn't break anything up, specially as he thinks it may not be suitable, but he'll speak to his wife, bows out, leaving the card where Sugar found it. And then—well, this is the part where we have to start guessing."

I just goggled at him. What on earth did the man think he'd been doing to date?

"What I mean," Crook said, "is the part we'll never be able to prove. Up to the time of Price's arrival we've got an independent witness, or will have when your boy's able to talk, which shouldn't be long from what the hospital was telling me. After that all we've got is Spurr's word, and if you think he's the strong silent type, you take it from the man who knows, he'll sing like a canary, and why shouldn't he, seeing there's no one to contradict his statement? Now, when he hears Price's car drive away he'll come down, leavin' your boy where no one, but no one, will think of lookin' for him. And—I told you this was where we start guessing —I'd say this is where he overplayed his hand. Y'see, he must know he can't marry the widow or even set up

ANTHONY GILBERT

house with her for a year, say. If the police don't drop
on him, the neighbors will. Annette ain't under suspicion, so far as he knows, and he can't turn her in,
even if he has a mind to, not without tying the rope
round his neck—well, you know what I mean. But he's
taken a lot of chances and it might, it just might, seem
to him he's got no guarantee they're goin' to pay off.
Or it could be he finds he's bitten off rather more than
he can chew. I don't say he'd have any pangs about
bumping Samson off, society ain't going to miss much
when he leaves the party, but this boy's different. For
one thing he's got a mum, and Spurr wasn't born
yesterday, he knows the one about the female of the
species bein' more deadly than the male.

"Well, he's got a good example under his eye, name
of Annette Samson. She's fixed her husband's murder,
and now there's the young chap who could be in the
way, no reason why she shouldn't pick Spurr for the
third corpse. Mind you, I don't think he ever expected
it 'ud come to that, but it must have gone through his
mind that at the year's end she might have melted away,
might even be Mrs. Someone Else. So it seems good
sense to get something on account. And that, I think, is
where Annette would produce *her* ace from *her* sleeve,
in the shape of the missing envelope. Might even have
taken a leaf out of your book, sugar, and deposited it
in the bank. Now if she's done that, we really might be
going places. Might have a word with Mall," he mused.
"Not that you don't have to get up pretty early in the
morning to get a bigger worm than him."

"So that's why the bedroom was torn to pieces? I
couldn't think why."

"Like I said," said Crook modestly, "it's all spec.
And it ain't up our street really, we don't have to find
out what happened, only the chap without curiosity gets
just nowhere."

208

"I do so Agree," cried Miss Muir eagerly. "Just think, if the prehistoric creatures had never wondered what it would feel like to walk upright, we might all be going about on all fours to this day."

"I knew you and me talked the same language," approved Crook. "Still, playing the Guessing Game, I'd say that's where Annette produced her little gun. She must have fired the first shot, police dug the cartridge out of the wall, then"—he shrugged his huge shoulders, giving the impression of rocks falling—"there was a shemozzle and we all know what happened to the second bullet. Any good lawyer would get him off on self-defense. Not that it 'ud help him much, he's got too much explaining to do."

"But why did he come and see Mrs. Ross?" asked Miss Muir. George had said nothing to date, just sat there like a dummy, but then he'd never been much of a talker. "My vocation's to write the epilogue," he told me once.

"If Philip hadn't given her his gun," I began, "she wouldn't have got shot."

"If ifs and ands were pots and pans—if the Lord God hadn't looked on His Work and seen that it was good we'd none of us be here today." Crook had a royal way of sweeping up objections; you couldn't help admiring it. "Anyway, you had it for a good many years and you never used it, and don't tell me there weren't times . . ."

George unexpectedly broke his silence. "When I shook in my shoes," he agreed.

"Now there's another thing I don't understand." Miss Muir persisted; she was having the time of her life. "Why did he come back to see Mrs. Ross?"

"Because he couldn't be sure she mightn't be dangerous to him, and he was too yellow to take a chance. Y'see, her boy had been told, say, it's your Mum wants you, and keep mum about it—but Spurr couldn't be certain he wouldn't just send her a p.c. Not to worry, he'd be back."

"You can't know my son very well if you think he spends any time writing p.c.'s to his mother," I assured him.

"Well, I don't, do I? What matters is, Spurr didn't know him either. He's got a good excuse for calling, still worried about the envelope, if questions should be asked."

"You wouldn't need to ask why anyone would want to call on Margaret," said old Angela Muir. "You know, it worried me. I knew that face—I don't say I never forget a face, not much compliment to faces if I did, they change like the weather, but there was something—it Haunted me. Then, when I saw the two of you together next day, the penny dropped. And I started to ask myself, What does this criminal want with Margaret Ross?"

"Must have shaken him when he heard Sugar had actually been to Virginia Water," said Crook buoyantly. "And then when she told him she was going down again—oh, the house was locked up, but he knew how many beans make five. A man would go home, shutters closed, milk stopped, no sign of life, but not a woman and certainly not a mum. And he knew what was there, he wouldn't dare let her go alone. I suppose he hoped he could persuade her it was a waste of time to try and get in, it was all to his advantage that way. Then, when Annette was found, as she was bound to be sooner or later, Big Sister here would remember her going down to Virginia Water on the Sunday. Odds are none of the locals saw her after the Saturday, and no one would have seen her since. So when the police came hunting with their little trident—Means, Motive and Opportunity—why, Spurr had it made. Her son conned, her gun on the premises . . ."

"Would I be expected to leave the premises without making sure my son wasn't there?" I demanded.

"We-ell, it don't seem like you'd go hunting in the attic. I mean, he wouldn't put himself there, and Annette was a ball of fluff, she'd never lug a fellow like your son up all those stairs. No, that 'ud be the irony, as these literates like to put it—there's you down below putting a bullet in the little lady while all the time the one you want is a couple of floors up."

"I felt," continued Miss Muir, pursuing her aim with a single-mindedness a World Cup player might have envied, "I'd never forgive myself if anything happened to you because of me being so dense."

"You cottoned on pretty fast where they were going once the penny had dropped," Crook congratulated her.

"Oh, I'm like you, Mr. Crook, I play my hunches. And then, dear"—she turned to me—"you were so obviously dressed to go to the country, and you did try to put me off the scent. And why should you do that if you weren't afraid I might guess you were going back?"

"Lady's logic," murmured Crook, but it seemed to make perfectly good sense to me.

"Would you have felt a bit silly if you'd arrived and found the house empty?" I asked.

"In that case, I should have thought it my duty to inform the police, in case they didn't know. No, my real problem was How to Get There. I mean, a car is so much quicker than a Green Line—and they don't run so very often, and there might be a walk the other end. I just had to pray for a Miracle." She paused. "I did think that if you weren't there, well, I was sure you had gone the day before, and I might be able to screw something out of Mrs. Samson."

"I've never been called a miracle before," said George complacently.

"Is that what happened?"

Miss Muir nodded her head like a mandarin. "When I opened my eyes There He Was, asking for Mrs. Ross."

"I felt as if a tornado had hit me," George confessed. "Before I knew what was happening we were in this car-rental office, and Angela here was hauling out banknotes as if she was the keeper of the mint . . ."

"I always believe in Being Prepared for Emergencies," Miss Muir explained. "And there was this nice chauffeur. I explained it might be a case of life and death, and he knew all the short cuts, being a Practiced Driver . . ."

"I ought to have thought of that," I interrupted, chagrined. "How Spurr knew them, too, unless he was accustomed to visiting there. He never asked a soul the way, and it's nearly as remote as Shangri-La."

"You can't be expected to think of everything," said George in soothing tones. That's the sort of remark that breaks up marriages.

"The car," I clamored. "The car outside Robin in the Straw. Are you going to tell me . . ."

"I told you at the time, dear," interposed Miss Muir reproachfully. "It was sheer accident. Well, naturally. What good would a corpse have been to a driver in the hurry he was in? Anyway, even an amateur murderer wouldn't have chosen to perpetrate a crime in front of quite so many witnesses. No, you slipped, you genuinely did."

I suppose one day the Recording Angel may have the nerve to question one of Angela Muir's statements, but the Recording Angel and I don't bat in the same league, and I knew if she said it was so, it was so. But I wasn't through.

"I still can't accept it," I burst out. "That *ordinary*

man, the kind you think would be so comfortable to live with . . ."

"They're all ordinary," said Crook, "that's their strength. Next time you have an hour to spare, sugar, you treat yourself to the Chamber of Horrors. There's a nice little lady there, wearing a nurse's gray cloak, nice rosy cheeks, leaning towards you, oh, so eager to help —name of Dyer. Ring a bell? Baby farmer of Reading. Bamboozled any number of young girls who got themselves landed with a Little Stranger and knew they couldn't hope for a job with that tied round their necks. Kind Mrs. Dyer—you leave him with me, dear, I'll find a happy home for him, just pay what you can. Five pounds? Well, ten would be better, but if five's all you've got—some of them went as high as fifty, I understand—now, you don't have to worry. I'll take care of him. She did, too. Found them all homes in the river, some in the Thames, some in the Kennet, always the same bit of tape round their necks—got so careless that one day she wrapped a body in a sheet of brown paper with her own address on it. But if you'd met her in the street you might be forgiven for thinking her middle name was Florence Nightingale . . ."

The phone rang and Crook answered it. "Think of everything, don't they?" we heard him say. "Yes, that's right, with me now. Of course she'll be able to prove it. Hold the line." He looked at me. "They've got Spurr, he can't think what they're talking about."

"Even he can't hope to talk himself out of this one," I protested.

"He'll have a damn good try," Crook told me, "and the burden of proof's still on the police."

I felt like whoever it was who was shot through by a ray of purest light serene.

"If he's never been to Boxwood, ask him how he explains the presence of his cigarette lighter—his monogrammed lighter—in a locked garage beside the house, and how I come to know it's there," I purred.

"I'll pass it on," said Crook. "You'll probably be in the neighborhood later in the day, seeing your lad, they're going to ring through here about the time." He beamed. "Knew you wouldn't let me down," he said.

"You don't change," George said to me. "You always had the last word."

"Well," said Crook, putting the receiver back on its rest when he'd completed his report, "that about wraps it up. Jam for the police, though why they shouldn't have to earn it instead of having it handed to them in a silver spoon . . ."

He was interrupted by the dauntless Miss Muir, leaning forward to score in the eighty-ninth minute of the game.

"I'm afraid it doesn't run to very much jam," she said. "I really don't see how you can help admiring the police, Mr. Crook. I mean, when you come to consider, they've been right all along the line. They said Spurr was guilty of the Samson murder, and now we know he is. Oh, I know they let him go for a time, but I'm not one of those who believe that second thoughts are best. I was convinced they wouldn't arrest him without Good Cause, and what's good enough for the police is Good Enough for me."

I don't think many people can have seen Mr. Crook absolutely winded, but we three saw it then. When he had got his breath back, he leaned toward her over the untidy desk.

"If I was a marrying man, honey," he told her, "I'd make you an offer for that. Anyone that can give me that kind of a surprise goes right to the top of the class. Still, things being the way they are, how about you being Big Sister and coming out to lunch?"

"That would be Just the sort of Miracle I've always

hoped for," she breathed. "Do you think—is it just possible—there might be a photographer Lurking? Mr. Crook and Friend—I've so often dreamed of being Friend to some Great Celebrity."

George did a most uncharacteristic thing. He leaned forward and kissed her on the cheek. "Heaven will lay one on," he promised solemnly. "It wouldn't dare not."

It was worthy of Crook himself.

The phone rang again. "Hospital," he reported as he hung up. "Your lad's come round, and you can see him at three o'clock for five minutes flat. Probably find the police waiting for you," he warned, "but a lady with a husband in attendance don't have to worry about that. Not that I wouldn't back you and Big Sister here against the whole blooming force."

He shrugged himself into a great ginger-colored ulster and slammed an abominable brown bowler on his head. Then he offered Miss Muir his arm with the grace of a Regency buck. I wouldn't have thought he could do it.

George watched them go. "Salute to a brave man!" he said reverently. "In his shoes and feeling the way he does, I'd run a hundred miles. Believe it or not, Meg, she really believes she can get him. And my money would be on her."

That was all we said about Miss Muir.

>>> If you've enjoyed this book and would like to discover more great vintage crime and thriller titles, as well as the most exciting crime and thriller authors writing today, visit: >>>

The Murder Room
Where Criminal Minds Meet

themurderroom.com